Two Guns
to Yuma

Also by Ed Gorman
in Large Print:

The Day the Music Died
Ghost Town
Vendetta
Wake Up Little Susie
Will You Still Love Me Tomorrow?
Branded
Breaking Up Is Hard to Do
Everybody's Somebody's Fool
Gun Truth
Lawless
Relentless
Ride into Yesterday
Save the Last Dance for Me
Trouble Man

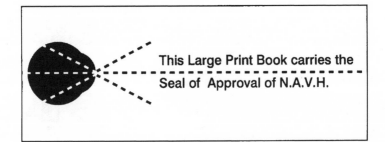

This Large Print Book carries the
Seal of Approval of N.A.V.H.

Two Guns to Yuma

Ed Gorman

Thorndike Press • Waterville, Maine

Published in 2005 by arrangement with
Dominick Abel Literary Agency Inc.

Thorndike Press® Large Print Western.

The tree indicium is a trademark of Thorndike Press.

The text of this Large Print edition is unabridged.
Other aspects of the book may vary from the original edition.

Set in 16 pt. Plantin by Ramona Watson.

Printed in the United States on permanent paper.

Library of Congress Cataloging-in-Publication Data

Gorman, Edward.
 Two guns to Yuma / by Ed Gorman.
  p. cm. — (Thorndike Press large print westerns)
 ISBN 0-7862-7742-4 (lg. print : hc : alk. paper)
 1. Sheriffs — Fiction. 2. Yuma (Ariz.) — Fiction.
3. Large type books. I. Title. II. Thorndike Press large
print Western series.
PS3557.O759T88 2005
 813'.54—dc22   2005009151

Two Guns to Yuma

National Association for Visually Handicapped
----------------------- serving the partially seeing

As the Founder/CEO of NAVH, the only national health agency solely devoted to those who, although not totally blind, have an eye disease which could lead to serious visual impairment, I am pleased to recognize Thorndike Press* as one of the leading publishers in the large print field.

Founded in 1954 in San Francisco to prepare large print textbooks for partially seeing children, NAVH became the pioneer and standard setting agency in the preparation of large type.

Today, those publishers who meet our standards carry the prestigious "Seal of Approval" indicating high quality large print. We are delighted that Thorndike Press is one of the publishers whose titles meet these standards. We are also pleased to recognize the significant contribution Thorndike Press is making in this important and growing field.

Lorraine H. Marchi, L.H.D.
Founder/CEO
NAVH

* Thorndike Press encompasses the following imprints: Thorndike, Wheeler, Walker and Large Print Press.

Prologue

Scared, opening first one blue eye then the other, he surveyed the hotel room with no recognition whatsoever. He might just as well have been on another planet. The room was shadowy, unknown.

In five minutes, he had raised himself no more than a few inches off the sway-backed mattress. Too much pain from the hangover. From the pounding headache. From the sweaty, feverish malaise that claimed his entire body. Not to mention the shakes. Oh God, the shakes.

Where the hell was he?

What the hell was he doing here?

He tried the easy things first. Name, Jeremy Hunt. Age, twenty-two. Occupation . . . now there was a joke. As the son of the valley's richest rancher, he had no occupation at all. Not unless you counted poker playing and beer guzzling.

Why did Lisa put up with him anyway?

Thinking of Lisa, he lay back down on the bed, fighting tears. He seemed determined to destroy their relationship. She'd given him chance after chance to grow up and be responsible for himself. But he always let her down. Always.

He wished Lisa were here with him now.

He felt so alone in the shadows of this room, moonlight silver and faint against the sheer curtains that moved like ghosts in the slight breeze.

Where the hell was he anyway?

And what the hell was he doing here?

Before he saw it, he smelled it, a sour odor emanating from somewhere in this room.

Propping himself up on his elbow again, he once more looked around. Bureau, wash basin, pitcher; easy chair with one broken leg canting it to the right; closet with the door slightly ajar.

From the closet.

That's where the sour odor was coming from.

What the hell was in the closet?

Getting up was more difficult than he could have imagined. The headache made any sort of movement intolerable. The dehydration made him tremble for a drink of water, which he would most likely vomit right back up. Then there was the raw anxiety over not knowing where he was. . . .

He went to the window, parted the curtains and looked down on a familiar street. Feeling relief, he put his head out into the night, letting the breeze touch him with fingers as soft as Lisa's.

This was Willow Creek, the town his father had helped build. The town where Jeremy Hunt was tolerated if not exactly respected. . . .

So he'd come to town on a bender and rented a hotel room to sleep it off. Something he often did. Too often.

Drawing fresh air into his lungs, he pulled himself back inside the room and decided he was strong enough to go to the closet.

He was two steps from the closet door when the knock came.

He glanced at himself, realizing that he wore only a pair of trousers, no shirt, no socks. Hurrying about, he grabbed a shirt hanging from the back of a chair and put it on. The shirt smelled of beer.

He opened the door to see Deputy Ron Sorenson standing there. Sorenson, a slender man with a face getting soft with middle age, came into the room with his usual air of quiet sadness. Ten years ago his three-year-old son had been trampled to death by a horse on Main Street. Sorenson, it was commonly believed, would never get over it. He'd seen it from four feet away. As usual, he smelled vaguely of liquor.

"Evening, Jeremy."

"Evening, Ron."

"I had some complaints a while ago."

"Complaints?"

"Seems some of the residents heard some screams. I tried to get over here half an hour ago but Clem Peterson's midwife took sick and I had to help Mrs. Glanding with the birth." Sorenson spoke in a tone that was almost cordial. Despite his long-standing feud with Jeremy's father — the same feud that Sheriff John T. Larson had — Sorenson seemed to hold no ill for Jeremy.

"I sure don't know anything about any screams, Ron."

"You mind if I come in and look around?"

"Guess not."

Sorenson fixed him with a jeweler's eye, as if searching for flaws. "You sleeping one off?"

"Guess I am."

"You should give that stuff up, son. Drinking like that never gained a man anything but grief." Sorenson apparently saw no irony in his words.

"I expect you're right."

Sorenson came into the room, his long Texas boots jangling with spurs. He went over to the bureau and put a match to the wick of the oil lamp.

Holding the lamp in front of him, a thin yellow light casting shadowy illumination into three of the room's four corners, Sorenson looked around. Obviously he saw nothing untoward.

Then he started sniffing. "You smell something?"

"Guess I do."

Still sniffing, Sorenson seemed confused by what he smelled. Then his blue eyes narrowed in displeasure and recognition.

Before Jeremy knew what was happening, Sorenson had slipped his Colt from his holster, pointed it at Jeremy, and said, "You go sit down in that chair over there, Jeremy."

"What?" said Jeremy, confused. With his hangover, understanding even simple commands was difficult. But this made no sense at all. What was the deputy so upset about all of a sudden?

"That chair, Jeremy. You go over and sit down."

"But —"

Sorenson reached out and put the cold

end of the Colt right into Jeremy's temple. "You give me any more backtalk, Jeremy, I'm going to knock you out. You understand?"

Jeremy felt as if he were ten years old. "Yessir," he muttered, feeling a panic and helplessness that threatened to overwhelm him, break him into unmanly tears right in front of his father's enemy.

He went over and sat down and watched as the deputy eyed the closet.

"You here alone tonight, Jeremy?"

"Yessir."

"You sure about that?"

"Sure, as I can be, I guess. I had a lot to drink." Both hands full, one with his Colt and the other with the oil lamp, Sorenson had to use the toe of his boot to push the closet door full open.

He stuck the lamp inside and looked around.

"You've got some real problems, Jeremy. Come here."

Suddenly, Jeremy didn't want to move. He didn't know what Sorenson had found in the closet, he just knew that whatever it was, it was going to be terrible.

And Jeremy was going to be blamed for it.

"I said come here."

"Yessir."

Shaking, his body covered with a sweat that was now the texture of glue, Jeremy managed to get to his feet and walk eight wobbly steps to the closet.

"Look inside," Sorenson said.

"I don't want to, Ron. Please."

"You do what I say, Jeremy. Look inside."

"No, please, I —"

Sorenson put the Colt to Jeremy's head again. "Now, you look inside, son. And right now."

When he saw what was in there, Jeremy fell to his knees, sobbing and pounding the wooden floor with useless fists.

At this point, Sorenson leaned down to him and said, "Come on, Jeremy. I'll take you over to the jail then somebody can go get your pa."

Instead of sounding angry, Sorenson sounded sorry for the kid.

"Come on, Jeremy," he said quietly. "No sense in hurting yourself anymore."

Still sobbing, Jeremy got slowly to his feet, keeping his back to the closet.

He sure didn't want to look in there again. He sure didn't.

Chapter One

Thursday, September 14, 1887
11:03 a.m.

Once again the dream troubled Cage's sleep. The same dream as always since the shooting three months ago. As usual Cage had shouted for his young deputy Les Jeter to turn around and fire to his left. But it was too late. In the dream, as in life, Jeter died.

Awake now, Richard Cage sat up and began rubbing his face. Memories of the funeral returned. Jeter's nineteen-year-old widow six months pregnant with their first child. Jeter's father, a Civil War vet suffering from palsy. Jeter's mother, a sad-eyed woman at the best of times, now melancholy in a way Cage could not look at long. All of them staring at him with blame and rage in their eyes as Cage made his way to the casket where he crossed himself and said some furtive prayers, their eyes never leaving his back. Sometimes, hatred could wound you more deeply than bullets. It had taken him to

14

age twenty-eight to find that out.

"Willow Creek," the conductor said, moving down the aisle of the Pullman. "We'll have a forty-five-minute stop here. Suggest you take the opportunity to stretch your legs and have yourself some dinner."

Cage stood up, a short, chunky man in a good white Western shirt, jeans, and a pair of well-shined brown boots. His brown eyes held both intelligence and a certain sorrow. His twice-broken nose revealed that he sometimes dealt with his sorrow through violence. This was why he was headed to Yuma — to start a new life.

Smiling at the two youngsters who'd been running up and down the aisle ever since the train had left yesterday, Cage made his way past the usual mix of train passengers — irritable mothers trying to control their broods, stoical Indians on their way to reservations, drummers sporting plaid shirts and vast nervous insincere smiles, and shabby gray old men who looked as if they were caught up in griefs so terrible words could not fittingly describe them. The car smelled of sweat, coffee, tobacco, and faintly, urine.

A few minutes later, Cage stood on the platform, appreciating the warm autumn air and the sight of a civilized town. Both telegraph and electrical wires cross-hatched the blue sky above; and in a few places, Cage even saw telephone lines. A horse-drawn trolley moved down the dusty main street, a merry tinkling bell sounding every few yards. Women in colorful dresses and picture hats stood in clusters chatting or pointing to store windows filled with a cornucopia of dry goods. Not only was Willow Creek civilized, it also seemed to be prosperous.

Cage jumped down from the platform and decided to have a better look for himself.

"He'll never hang."

"He did it, didn't he?"

"He did it, all right. But they'll never hang him. Not Art Hunt's kid they won't. Hell, Hunt won't even let 'em get the kid on the train tomorrow morning."

"How's he gonna stop 'em?"

"You know Hunt, don't you? He'll stop 'em any way he needs to."

For lunch Cage had a ham sandwich and a cup of coffee. He tried hard to resist the slice of pumpkin pie the coffee shop owner had showed him but he couldn't.

The coffee shop was crowded with people who worked in town, laborers with

16

denim overalls and sunburns and scraped-up knuckles and shop clerks with pomaded hair and colorful shoulder garters on their sleeves and a slight air of superiority whenever their eyes set on the laborers.

The two men talking about some kid named Jeremy Hunt sat at the counter next to Cage. The word "hanging" won Cage's attention right away, but even after two minutes of eavesdropping, he still had no idea of what they were really talking about.

He finished up the pie along with a fresh cup of coffee. According to his pocket Ingram, he had ten minutes to get back to the train. That was a joke, of course. The way trains ran, he'd be lucky if it pulled out within an hour.

The taller man of the two talkers said, "You wait and see, Art Hunt'll do something today. They'll never get Jeremy on the train."

"Where they takin' him anyway?"

"Cedar County. Figure he'd never get a fair trial around here — the jury'd be afraid to convict him."

The shorter of the two men shook his head. "Young punk. 'Bout time he got his."

Cage paid his tab and left, still curious about the "young punk" the two men were discussing. Cage had the natural interests of a longtime lawman plus he liked gossip the same as anybody else.

In the street, he stepped around some fly-busy road apples, sighted a very pretty woman who showed total disinterest in him, and started to work his way back to the depot along a side street that belonged mostly to the kind of tavern where traveling railroad crews drank — in other words, tough places that young lawmen soon learned to be leery of. He'd had both his nose and his head smashed open in just such places. Sometimes badges didn't mean a whole hell of a lot.

As he reached the mouth of an alley, something on the periphery of his vision troubled him. He turned just in time to see a man hunched behind a large wooden barrel. The man was sighting along a rifle.

The situation was much like the one that had gotten young Jeter killed.

Turning quickly to his left — the whole incident taking place in a matter of seconds — Cage saw a tall man in a dark, three-piece suit striding down the middle of the dusty street. He walked with an almost arrogant manner, eyes scanning about. Only too late did he see the man behind the barrel.

Cage dove for the assassin just as the

man prepared to fire. For the first time, Cage wondered if his decision to no longer carry a gun had been a wise one. All he could do now was throw himself in the direction of the would-be killer and —

The shot struck the tall man anyway, getting him in the shoulder. The tall man dropped the gun he'd been drawing and fell over backward on the street. Cage, who had collided with the assassin, scrambled to his feet.

The man behind the barrel lifted his rifle and pointed it at Cage. "You're messin' where you don't belong, pardner." Like Cage, the man was short and chunky. Unlike Cage, he needed a shave, a bath, and some new clothes. "Now you just wait right there till I get a chance to get out of this alley. You hear me?"

There was no point in arguing, Cage knew. Behind him, he could hear people shouting, running toward the fallen man.

The gunman looked frustrated. "If I hurt him bad, it's your fault."

"What?" Cage said. Had he heard the man right? If the man hadn't been trying to hurt the fallen man — then what was he doing crouching in the alley?

But Cage wasn't to get an answer to his question. The gunman backed down the alley till he reached the end of it then he ducked behind a barn and disappeared.

Knowing there was no point in pursuing the gunman, Cage ran to the street, where townspeople had formed a small circle around the fallen man.

Only when he reached the man did Cage see the silver, five-pointed star the man wore on the lapel of his suitcoat. While the rest of the sheriff's clothes were dusty from the street, the badge shone with an almost eerie light.

"How is he?" Cage asked.

"Not near as bad as some people would wish I was." The answer came not from one of the onlookers but from the lawman himself. "Now, Buck, you give me your hand and help me to my feet and the rest of you quit making a fuss, all right? If I can live through my wife's cooking, I can sure live through a little gunshot."

The townspeople smiled. A burly man named Buck put out a wide slab of hand and helped raise the lawman to his feet.

"May I have your name, sir?" the lawman said to Cage.

Cage told him.

"I'm in your debt."

Cage shrugged. "Not really. You'd have

done the same thing for me."

The lawman squinted his blue eyes. At first, Cage thought that the squint reflected the man's pain. Beneath a wide tear in the man's coat, Cage could see the shoulder beneath, the glimpse of blood, bone, and flesh. This was one tough lawman.

"You're in the same business I am," the sheriff said.

"What?"

"Your business. It's being a lawman, isn't it?"

Cage felt himself flush. "Well it used to be anyway."

"Thought so."

The man put forth his one good hand. Cage shook it. "I'm John T. Larson, sheriff of these parts." He looked at the still-anxious townspeople and smiled. "These good folks have seen fit to renew my contract four times. That makes near thirty years."

Larson was a splendid showman. You could gauge his effectiveness in the awe on the faces of the crowd. Anybody else would be lying on some doc's table getting the bullet dug out by now. But Larson, tall, handsome in a craggy sort of way, was standing here spreading good cheer.

"You'd better head over to the hospital," one of the townspeople said.

"Doesn't that sound nice?" Larson said to Cage. " 'The hospital'? Sisters of Mercy just erected it last year. Seventeen beds and its own surgery." He glanced around dramatically, his Stetson pointing out the various two- and three-story buildings that could be seen a block behind these false fronts. "Seventeen beds and a surgery. Now is Willow Creek a wonderful town or not?"

Larson stared right at Cage, demanding an answer. "Sure looks that way to me," Cage said, feeling his cheeks heat up again. "Uh, wonderful, I mean."

Larson reached out and grabbed him then and pulled him tight to his chest. Cage's head barely reached Larson's watch pocket. Larson addressed the crowd rather than Cage. "This, folks, is the son I never had." He relished the phrase and repeated it. "Yes, the son I never had."

Cage could imagine women swooning and strong men weeping over such hokum.

Abruptly, Larson released Cage from his iron grip, sort of flinging him back a few steps.

To the crowd Larson said, "Is this not a fine town, my good people?"

"Oh, yes," several people said — "Oh, yes!" — as if they were answering a Baptist minister.

"Did Cage here get a good look at him, Sheriff?" said a man in the crowd. "The man who shot you, I mean?"

John T. Larson waved his hat again. "All in good time, Lester; all in good time. I'm sure that Mr. Cage and I will have many things to discuss in the next few hours."

Cage started to say that he had to get back to the depot and catch a train but Larson didn't give him a chance.

"Tonight, I plan to buy Mr. Cage here the best steak in town, as well as a good bottle of Kentucky mash, and to show him the hospitality that only this wonderful town has to offer. How does that sound, Mr. Cage?"

Cage was about to tell Larson about the train but Larson grabbed him again in another dramatic hug. Cage felt his ribs bruise. The guy was a goddamn bear.

"Now, why don't you good folks let Mr. Cage escort me to the hospital, and then I can get on with the business of law and order?"

"I don't know how you do it, John T.," one man said reverently, and several others gushed and whispered similar pieces of praise.

Larson used Cage as his crutch, draping his bad arm over Cage but never breaking his magnificent — and arrogant — stride.

Behind them the praise and well-wishes of the crowd floated on the warm autumn day like bright balloons.

They were just out of earshot when John T. Larson said, "You stupid little prick, couldn't you have jumped him sooner so that he wouldn't have got a shot at me?"

Chapter Two

The hospital smelled crisply of antiseptic. Cage sat in an uncomfortable leather chair outside a small operating room. He kept rolling himself cigarettes and looking at the big Ingram on the wall. He was long past his train. He supposed there was no rational reason he couldn't go into the operating room and just tell Sheriff John T. Larson that he was leaving Willow Creek and that if Larson didn't like it, the hell with him.

The longer he sat there, the more he resented the big man's attitude, as if Cage were his deputy.

To hell with him indeed.

He was going up where grazing land was green and a man could forget all about being a lawman and seeing a young deputy backshot.

He stood up, stretched, put on his hat, and started down the narrow corridor toward the front door. This being a Catholic hospital, the walls were lined with religious paintings. Even though he was a Lutheran, Cage decided to take his hat back off. It

25

didn't hurt to be friendly, even to someone else's god.

"Oh, Mr. Cage."

The voice was sweet as birdsong, and when he turned, he was surprised to see a middle-aged nun hurrying toward him, her black and white habit very starchy and clean looking.

"Afternoon, Sister," Cage said, nodding.

"You're not leaving, are you, Mr. Cage?"

"Well, I kind of thought I was, Sister. To be frank and all."

"Oh, but Sheriff Larson specifically asked that we keep you here."

"Oh, he did, did he?"

"Yes. He said you're going to help him."

"Help him?" Cage said, thoroughly confused. "Help him what?"

"Why help him make sure that Arthur Hunt doesn't try and break his son Jeremy out of jail." The nun's homely but friendly face beamed. "And Willow Creek is very appreciative, too, Mr. Cage. You volunteering and all." She pointed back to the chair where Cage had been sitting. "Now why don't you go sit there again until the doctor finishes with Sheriff Larson. In the meantime, I'll bring you some cookies and milk."

"Cookies and milk?" Cage said, feeling

as though he were eight years old.

"Chocolate chip cookies," the nun said. "I made them myself, and if you'll forgive some immodesty on my part, I must say they're very good."

She took his shoulder and turned him back in the direction of the chair. "Now you go sit there and I'll be along shortly."

Eight years old — no two ways about it.

The operating room was white. So was the bed on which Sheriff Larson lay. Or had been. Now the sheets up by his shoulder were stained red with blood. The doctor said, "Too bad the sonofabitch got your shooting arm, John T."

The doctor, a stout man in a brown vest and matching pants and a rumpled white shirt without a collar, scrubbed his hands at a basin. When he saw Cage come in, he said, "Sure do appreciate the help you're going to give this town, Mr. Cage. I sure do." Then the doctor looked into a small hanging mirror. He seemed to be admiring the fact that he was in need of a shave. The doctor turned back to Cage and put out his hand. "I'm Reames, John T.'s cousin."

"Nice to meet you," Cage said, shaking hands.

"Now this wild bastard is going to try and tell you that he's fine and that he can be up and around in no time. You understand?"

Cage shrugged. "Sure. I guess."

"But don't believe him."

"Don't?"

"Nope. He didn't suffer a fatal wound but he suffered a serious one and he needs bed rest. You're going to have to cover all his duties yourself."

"I am?"

"Yes, and again, Mr. Cage, it was damn nice of you to volunteer."

"But —"

Dr. Reames went over and patted Larson on his good shoulder. "I'm leaving this crazy sonofabitch in your hands, Mr. Cage." He waggled a school-teacherish finger at Cage. "And I'm holding you personally responsible for his well-being."

"You are?"

Dr. Reames seemed to hear none of the hesitancy and confusion — not to mention irritation — in Cage's voice. "I'm sure you'll do fine," Dr. Reames said. His dark, friendly eyes scanned Cage up and down. "Kind of a little feller, aren't you?"

"I do all right for myself."

"Oh, don't take offense, Mr. Cage, because none was intended." He patted Larson on his good shoulder once again. "I

28

just mean that around here we're used to our lawmen being kind of giant-sized."

Nodding to Cage, Dr. Reames left the operating room.

Cage decided to get control of himself before he spoke. He had one of those tempers that lent itself to explosions.

"You look pissed off, kid," Larson said.

"Don't call me kid."

"Just trying to be friendly."

"What's the idea of telling everybody that I'm going to help you out? I'm taking the next train out of here."

"Hell, I thought I was doing you a favor."

"A favor?"

"Sure. Giving you a chance to redeem yourself."

"Redeem myself?"

"Kid, if you'd been quicker, that gunman wouldn't have shot me at all."

Cage felt his face heat up. "I may have saved your damned life. Did that ever occur to you?"

"Oh sure, it occurred to me but then I thought it over and decided nah, you didn't save my life."

"Nah?"

"Nope — because even if you hadn't been there, I would have spotted him and killed him."

"Are you crazy? Why, if I hadn't been there —"

"Kid, what's the point in arguing? Neither one of us can be sure you actually saved my life. All we *can* be sure of is that you weren't quick enough to save me from getting wounded." Sheriff John T. Larson shook his magnificent theatrical head. "Now, no offense, kid, but if I was you, I'd be kind of embarrassed about this whole thing."

Cage stood there watching and listening in disbelief. Here he'd gone and saved a man's life and now the man was telling him that he should be "embarrassed."

"And that's exactly why I gave you this opportunity to redeem yourself." He shook his head again. "You don't want to leave Willow Creek with your head hanging low, do you? Of course not. You want to walk out of here proud and pleased with yourself. Leaving a good memory behind. Now, kid, I can see by your eyes that you know exactly what I'm talking about. I can see it right there in those brown eyes of yours. That's one of the things I'm good at, reading people's eyes." He pointed to his ragged, bloody shirt and a small black leather case sitting next to it. "Hand me one of those cigars, would you, kid?"

"No."

"No?" Now it was John T. Larson's turn to look disbelieving.

"No. Not until you hear me out."

"Now isn't that a fine howdy-do? The kid won't give me one of my own cigars." The lawman seemed to be addressing some ghostly presence only he could see.

"For Christ's sake," Cage said, too late recalling that he was in a Catholic hospital, "here." He grabbed the black case and slammed it on the bed next to Larson. "Now you listen to me."

"All right, kid. All right." But already Larson's attention was mostly given over to getting a fine brown-leafed cigar from the case. It was not easy to do — open the case, draw the cigar out from its slotted resting place — but John T. Larson managed. He shoved the cigar in his mouth, bit off the end with a certain fastidiousness, and then expelled it with great force into a wastebasket halfway across the room. "Now go ahead, kid."

"I'm leaving here and I'm finding myself a hotel room and I'm getting me some newspapers and maybe a book and I'm going to sit in that hotel room until it's time for my train to come and then I'm going to get on that train and get the hell out of here. I've missed one train and I don't plan to miss another. And I don't give one good damn what happens to Jeremy Hunt or anybody else in this burg, do you understand?"

"How about lighting this cigar for me, kid?"

"My God," Cage said. "You didn't hear a word I said, did you?"

"Kid, you've got a problem."

"What?"

"A problem. Seeing's how I've told several people that you're going to help me out, and seeing's that they in turn told several people and so on and so forth, most of the people in this 'burg' as you call it are under the impression that you're going to help out their poor old shoulder-shot sheriff. And if you don't, kid, you're going to look pretty doggoned bad, kid. Pretty doggoned bad." He stuck his cigar out and said, "Now how about that light?"

Chapter Three

She had never broken into anybody's room before.

Lisa Tate stood at the bottom of the wooden stairs that ran at an angle up the rear of the Savory Hotel. In the sunshine of the warm day, she could plainly see the scabbed paint, the cracked windows, and the ragged window screens that helped mark the Savory for what it was — a decidedly second-rate hotel frequented by luckless drummers, drifters, and old folks who couldn't afford to live anywhere else.

Lisa put a trembling hand on the banister and started the steep ascent to the third floor. A slender woman with long, chestnut hair that appeared a fiery red in the sunlight, Lisa was not by ordinary standards beautiful. Yet her face was so animated, her brown eyes so knowing and playful, that her pretty features took on a real beauty. By the time she'd turned twenty-three, which was just this past sum-me, Lisa had broken too many hearts to keep score.

But now it was a different Lisa Marie

Tate climbing the stairs. In her right hand, clutched tight as a schoolgirl's valentine, was a key that would let her into Room 317. In her purse was a Navy Colt. Though her father and two brothers had raised her to be a good shot, she was not sure that she could actually fire a gun at another person.

By the time she reached the first section of the third floor, moving past doors behind which she heard snoring, coughing, cursing, and — far down the hall — vomiting, Lisa had nearly convinced herself that she could not go through with it.

What if she got caught? Imagine the humiliation her mother would endure if her daughter was arrested for breaking and entering.

Just before she opened the door leading to the second section of the third floor, she paused at a window and looked down into the dusty alley below her. In the west corner, a small boy and girl played hide and seek in a storage barn. She thought of how she and her own brothers used to play similar games in similar alleys. Life used to be so much simpler. How had it ever gotten this complicated?

She turned back to the door, opened it on creaking hinges, and went inside.

The hallway was dark and smelled of whiskey and tobacco and a few other things Lisa didn't like to think about.

The key seemed to burn in her hand.

Glancing around her, she saw that all the doors on both sides of the corridor were closed. From behind them came various guttural sounds of people getting up for the day. At this time, early afternoon, it meant they were most likely waking to terrible hangovers. Shaking her head with stern disapproval, she moved down the corridor.

The room she wanted was near the end of the corridor. Dust motes floated in a beam of warm sunshine pouring through a skylight. A plump gray tomcat lazed in the light, opening one eye to peer up at the woman who'd wakened him. He seemed impressed with her.

A cat lover, Lisa's first instinct was to bend down, scratch him under the chin, and start up a conversation. Lisa spent hours conversing with her own cats, which presently numbered six, a figure that would probably double when beautiful Emmaline gave birth to her brood.

But, she told herself sternly, there was no time for cat conversations this afternoon. She was here, after all, in the capacity of a burglar.

After checking first one way then the other, and then saying a quick silent prayer, she fitted the key to the lock and felt something like shock when the door opened so readily.

She stood in the hall, her heart hammering so loudly she could not even hear the hungover men cough and quake anymore.

Here.

Now.

The moment had arrived.

She pushed inside quickly then closed the door quietly behind her.

Her first feeling, on surveying the small room, was sadness.

How awful it would be to live out your years in such a dark, drab little room. The double bed was unmade, bedclothes hanging off the sway-back mattress and even trailing to the floor. The bureau mirror was cracked very badly down the middle and two bureau drawers were missing, like teeth in a youngster's mouth. The easy chair was absent part of a leg and sat at a comic angle that seemed to dare anybody to sit in it. In one corner was a heap of sour-smelling dirty clothes running to shirts and underwear and in another corner a collection of half-eaten dinners brought up from the restaurant next door presumably, food encrusted on all the plates, and cockroaches the size of small fingers crawling all over the plates. Everything was dusty and broken in some way and she could not help her depression. Whatever she might think of Sam Jenkins, the hotel manager, living out life in this room seemed similar to a prison sentence.

She had no idea where to begin.

She had no idea what she was even looking for.

Something.

Anything.

Or else Jeremy would —

So she began, first systematically through the bureau drawers where several times she had to pause, the sadness overcoming her again, for she'd never thought of somebody as despicable and immoral as Sam Jenkins having a family — yet here they were. Photographs of a sweet old couple who were obviously his parents standing on the steps of a little house that actually looked much more like a shack. Even photographs of Sam himself, his arm around a pleasant-looking if very hefty young woman who was holding a baby. Probably Sam's baby. Given what she knew about Sam, he'd probably deserted both the woman and the child.

But nothing — nothing useful at all to be found in any of the drawers.

She next turned to the closet, which smelled of moth balls and dampness, almost as if she were entering a cave.

There were three cheap suits hanging there and she deftly went through the pockets of each one, finding abundant amounts of lint, chewing gum, lint, lucifers, and cigarette papers.

Just as her fingers touched on something interesting — what felt like an envelope — she heard the footsteps and the voices in the corridor.

My God.

What if it was Sam Jenkins?

What if he found her in here?

Snatching the envelope from the interior pocket of the suitcoat, she jumped into the closet and quickly pulled the door shut. The sound of her pounding heart filled the darkness of the tiny room. She had to stand rigidly; if she moved, she'd nudge against the empty wire hangers behind her and they'd clang like bells.

Gruff male laughter.

Heavier footsteps.

Key in lock.

Turning —

My God it really was —

Sam Jenkins.

"You think you're ever gonna clean up this pig sty, Sammy?" a crude female voice said.

"Sure — as soon as your madame hires you girls out for housework."

The woman laughed. "I'd rather make my living on my back than on my knees doing housework."

Rustle of clothes; obviously Sam Jenkins had pulled the woman closer to him. "I'm glad you feel that way, Edie. I'm real glad." More rustling of clothes; then the wet sucking sounds of very earnest and passionate kissing.

My God, Lisa was going to have to hide in a closet and listen to Sam Jenkins have a tryst with a prostitute. My God.

"We gotta do this fast," Sam Jenkins said. "I gotta go to the goddamn dentist's this afternoon."

Edie laughed. "With you, Sam, it's always fast."

"Didn't used to be."

Edie kept teasing him. "Sure, Sam. That's what they all say."

Apparently, Jenkins didn't mind her teasing. "It's true. I used to be a real hellion in bed. Then I turned forty — Well guess I'm just gettin' older."

Lisa could hear the prostitute getting out of her clothes. "You should try some of that Doc Forbes Elixir I take."

"Yeah?"

"Yeah."

Now Lisa could hear Sam Jenkins, who was about eighty or ninety pounds overweight, getting out of his own clothes.

The bed squeaked.

"God, Edie, I sure do like your tits."

"Couldn't you call 'em breasts once in a while?"

"Oh, yeah, I forgot. Breasts."

There was a silence as the bedsprings squeaked a little more. "I better get a little wet first," Edie said. "It'll be better for both of us."

"You want me to do it?"

"Nah, I'll do it myself."

A terrible panic had befallen Lisa. She felt she was not being true to her principles by standing here and listening to people talk this way. But she couldn't even so much as plug her ears because simply by raising her arms she'd set the wire hangers to clanging.

But God, the language was so vile —

She just hoped that if she and Jeremy ever got married they'd never lose so much respect for each other that they'd talk this way.

Sam Jenkins and Edie began making love.

Jenkins grunted a few times and then he sounded really out of breath.

And then it was over.

Just like that.

Lisa could hear him rolling off the bed. "You sure earned some easy money today," Jenkins said.

Lisa could hear Jenkins climbing into his pants. The zipper made some very loud noise in the sad little dusty room.

"You really should try some of that elixir," Edie said, rolling off the bed and rustling into her own clothes now.

"You really think it'd help?" Jenkins said.

"It helps me."

"Honest?"

"Sure. I used to fall asleep when I was with some customers. Now I stay awake almost all the time." Edie laughed. "Though falling asleep may have been a blessing in disguise."

"You ever get tired of what you do?"

"What else *could* I do? I don't know nothin' else, Sam. I came out here for the gold camps when I was fourteen. 'Bout the only thing that's left for me now."

41

Lisa could hear Sam Jenkins thumb a lucifer into a minor explosion. In moments, cheap rancid cigar smoke lay on the air.

"C'mon," Jenkins said, "I got to be gettin' to the dentist."

"Don't pay me in change this time, all right, Sam? I hate it when you pay me in change. Pay me in greenbacks, all right?"

Then they were at the front door and going out. "So where do I get some of this elixir?" Sam Jenkins said right before the door closed.

Lisa stood in the closet long after she could have snuck out. She was stunned by all of it — sneaking in then having to hide out then hearing that strange sad conversation between Jenkins and the prostitute. Instead of making her hate Jenkins all the more, the conversation had made her feel sorry for him.

Slowly, she eased the closet open and set one foot out into the room.

And it was just then that the hotel door burst open and Sam Jenkins stood there, glaring at her.

Before she could even think of digging into her purse and pulling out the Colt, Jenkins's hand was filled with his own Colt.

"Just what the hell are you doing in my room?" he said.

Looking meaner than he ever had before — big, swarthy, vaguely unclean — he started across the room toward her.

"Answer me, you little bitch," he said. "Answer me right now."

Chapter Four

The sheriff's office was a large, two-story redbrick building on a busy corner two doors down from the livery and the blacksmith. Above the front door, in bold black letters against a white field, a sign read SHERIFF JOHN T. LARSON, ESQUIRE. Cage smiled to himself when he saw this. The splendiferousness of the ESQUIRE revealed a great deal about Larson.

This was the first time Cage had smiled in more than two hours. He had still not quite recovered from the easy way he'd been dragged into this whole mess. Larson explained it as "fate." Cage thought "bad luck" was more like it.

Pushing open the door, Cage smelled immediately the aroma of hot coffee brewing. Then of pipe tobacco. His first impression of the office was that it was got up to resemble a business office and not a sheriff's office at all. Behind a low railing with a swing door sat two rows of desks, three deep. Behind these were four wooden filing cabinets that appeared to be brand new. To the right was a massive oak rolltop desk with a fancy brass name-plate sitting on the top that repeated the SHERIFF JOHN T. LARSON motif. To the left was a barred window through which came smoky autumn sunlight.

Two desks down, the right row, sat a tall, slim man with graying hair. He worked with his head down signing a stack of forms. His haste and his occasional tongue-clucking revealed his distaste for forms, a distaste Cage, too, always felt. If he had heard Cage come in, the man didn't let on. He continued to write furiously, turning over a new form every few seconds.

"Excuse me," Cage said, his voice loud on the lazy, smoky air.

When the man looked up, Cage's first thought was that he'd never seen a sadder pair of eyes, not even on men who knew they would soon be going to the gallows.

"Help you?" the gray-haired man said.

"My name's Cage."

"Oh. Right," the man said, standing up from his desk and coming up the small aisle. He put out his hand. His grip was not particularly strong but then Cage wasn't concerned with the grip. He was still concerned about the man's eyes. What the hell could have happened to make a man look this bad? This close, he noticed another thing, too. The faint but unmistakable odor of whiskey on the man's breath. "Ron Sorenson. Deputy Ron Sorenson. You sure came in handy today. The town's very appreciative."

"Not according to the sheriff, I didn't," Cage said. "According to him, he wouldn't have been shot at all if I hadn't pushed the man out of the way."

Sorenson smiled, or tried to anyway. With those eyes, a smile didn't look real convincing on that face. "Oh hell, Cage, don't get riled about that. That's just John T.'s way. He hates to admit that he owes anybody anything. I've been with him twelve years here. He's a good man except that he lets his vanity get in the way sometimes. You know — John T. Larson admitting that he had to let somebody else help save his life? That isn't the kind of thing John T. would ever own up to is all."

Cage looked around. "Where are the men?"

"Men?"

"Larson told me that a man named Coggins was rounding up some deputies in case this Arthur Hunt decides to storm the office here and try and get his son back."

"You pitching in? Is that the deal?" Sorenson said. He sounded happy about such a prospect.

Cage shook his head. "No. I just told Larson I'd simply check things out and see how they were going."

"Larson tells me you're a lawman."

"Was a lawman, to be precise."

"Give it up?"

"Yep. I'm on my way to my brother's ranch. I'm going to work with cattle the rest of my life instead of human beings. And I'm going to be one hell of a lot happier." Cage sniffed coffee. "Mind if I have a cup?"

"Help yourself."

Cage went over and picked up a white glass mug and filled it with steaming brown liquid from a gray metal coffee pot. "So where are the special deputies this Coggins is supposed to line up?"

"Coggins isn't back yet."

"Who is he anyway?"

"Haberdasher. He's pretty active in civic affairs in these parts. Decent enough man if a little bit proud of himself."

Cage grinned. "He and Larson must get along fine." He sipped hot, strong, tasty coffee. "Jeremy Hunt back there?"

"Right."

"You checked on him lately?"

"Half hour or so, I guess."

"Mind if I take a gander?"

"Hell no. Wish you would. It's going to be a long eighteen hours till the train shows up and takes Jeremy to Cedar County. Especially with John T. laid up. My understanding is that he can't shoot."

Cage sipped more coffee. "It's worse than that. Not only can't he shoot, he can't walk."

Horror showed in Sorenson's gaze. "He's paralyzed?"

"No, just kind of dizzy. Larson doesn't want to let on, of course, but at his age a wound like that is nothing to trifle with. We helped him up on his feet and he didn't make it three feet. He collapsed. The wound has taken a lot out of him."

"Poor old guy," Sorenson said sincerely. "This has to really hurt his pride."

"Cell block door open?"

"Yep."

"Thanks."

Cage put down his cup and walked over to a massive wooden door that had been reinforced with slabs of steel. Creaking open, the door let go cooler, dank air, the sort you could imagine coming from a crypt. The cell block, three cells on each side, was dark. The only patch of sunlight was in the small windows set high on the wall of each cell. You could smell chewing tobacco and urine. A red Indian lay on the nearest bunk snoring. As he passed by the man, Cage could smell the sour odor of hangover. All the other cells were empty except one, the last one on the right. On the cot in that one a medium-sized young man who might have been handsome if he weren't so pale and washed-out lay on his bunk staring at the ceiling and muttering to himself. Anyway, that was Cage's first impression. When he got closer, he saw that the kid had a black rosary coiled in his slender white hand. The kid was praying.

"Afternoon," Cage said when he reached the last cell.

The kid quit praying and looked up. "You a new attorney or something?"

"Nope. Just kind of inspecting things."

"Oh. You must be one of those special deputies Larson is trying to scare up."

"Sort of, I guess." He stared hard at the kid. Good, intelligent features and an air of intelligence and refinement that might be feminine in another such kid. But this kid looked sturdy enough. He just looked scared.

Jeremy Hunt sat up, his brown hair uncombed and wild about his head. He wore a wrinkled blue jail shirt and wrinkled blue jail pants. "You seen Lisa Tate?"

"Who?"

"You don't know Lisa?"

"Afraid I don't."

"She was supposed to come see me. She was supposed to be here half an hour ago."

Cage raised his eyes to a word the kid had scratched deep into the stone wall: LISA, written huge. Just the size of the name told you about the plaintiveness the kid felt for the girl. "Maybe she just got detained."

The kid smiled sourly. "Well she ain't got long to get detained, mister. In case you haven't heard, they're taking me away in the morning."

Cage nodded.

The kid stood up and came over to the bars. He kept his rosary in his right hand, clutching it with a desperation that made Cage sad. That was the hell of it about people who got in trouble, even some murderers — no matter how much you wanted to hate them for what they'd done, you still found them pretty sad as people. For that reason, Cage had always felt that sometimes hanging was a mercy. You took some poor bastard out of his misery — and out of society so he couldn't inflict his misery on others.

"I didn't do it," the kid said.

"I'm afraid I can't help you."

"I've thought about that night again and again and I know I didn't do it."

"You were drunk?"

The kid lowered his gaze. "So what if I was?"

"Sometimes people do things when they're drunk that they forget all about in the morning."

"You don't murder somebody and forget about that."

"I've known it to happen, kid. I'm sorry but that's the truth."

The kid raised his eyes again. "Well, I know that I didn't kill that girl. How's that? Is that good enough? That I know — despite how things look — that I didn't kill that girl." He was shouting and on the verge of tears.

Cage said softly, "That's a nice rosary."

His words seemed to calm the kid. "Right now, this is the only friend I've got." He scowled. "Where's Lisa? She promised she'd be here."

Cage said, "I'll go check."

He turned away from the kid and started back toward the cell block door. By now the red Indian was awake and standing up. He grinned at Cage. "Arthur Hunt's s'posed to have all this power but there his kid sits same as me." He laughed and then fell into a tobacco cough.

Cage went out of the block and closed the door behind him, grateful for the warm sunlight and the good clean smell of coffee again. It was like dying and going to heaven.

Sorenson sat perched on the edge of the low railing. He was talking to a stout man in a three-piece business suit. When he saw Cage, Sorenson said, "Mr. Cage, this is Havers Coggins."

Coggins put out a warm fleshy hand. Cage shook it.

"Ron here was just explaining to me who you are," Coggins said. When he spoke, it was with a precision that bordered on the ludicrous, like a stage actor trying to project to the rear of the theater. "And I'm afraid I've got bad news for you. Looks like you're going to be our acting sheriff."

"Mr. Coggins here couldn't get any special deputies," Sorenson said.

"Everybody's afraid of Art Hunt," Coggins explained. "Everybody." He shook his gray-streaked head more with anger than sadness. "I'd get involved myself but

I've been called out of town on a business trip."

Cage thought this was pretty convenient, getting called away at this time. His suspicions were confirmed when the deputy looked over at him and winked.

Coggins stood up. "But I'm sure things will be fine left in your capable hands, Mr. Cage."

He then punched Cage on the arm manfully and strode over to the front door. "I'll be back sometime tomorrow afternoon and you can give me a full report then."

Tomorrow afternoon, Cage thought. And Jeremy Hunt will either be on that train or Sorenson and I here will be dead. Thank you very much, Mr. Coggins.

"You boys take things easy now," Coggins said, and went out the door.

"Sure is too bad Coggins got called away," the deputy said. "Otherwise he would have been right here with us."

Cage smiled. "Seems that everybody in this town got called away." He nodded to the door leading to the cell. "It also seems it's going to be me and you."

"You're going to help me out?"

"Doesn't look as if I've got much choice."

The deputy laughed. "Well, the worst

thing that can happen to you is that you'll get shot by one of Hunt's men."

"What's the best thing that can happen to me?"

Sorenson grinned. "That your train will come early and you'll be out of here before the shooting starts."

And with that, Sorenson pulled open a drawer, pulled out a five-pointed star, and tossed it over to Cage. "Figure you'll need a badge," Sorenson said.

Pinning the badge on to his shirt, Cage thought of how far away his brother's Yuma ranch seemed. He thought of young Jeter getting killed, a death that may well have been Cage's fault.

Who was Richard Cage going to get killed this time?

Chapter Five

Lisa Tate said, "You're not going to shoot, are you?"

"I'm damned tempted to. Just what the hell are you doing in my room?" Sam Jenkins said.

Hours seemed to have passed from the time Jenkins came back to his room and found Lisa leaving his closet. But Lisa knew it had been only moments. Very long moments.

Lisa sighed. "Why don't you just let me go, Sam?"

"You didn't answer my question. What're you doing here?"

She had no idea what to say. Her mind was wild with vagrant thoughts but none seemed worth repeating aloud. She said, "Looking for something that would help Jeremy."

There. The truth. Hadn't she always been taught that the truth was best?

"And just what the hell is that supposed to mean?" Sam Jenkins said. As always, the overweight hotel manager looked tired and disheveled. His eyes were red and his skin was the color of a worm's underbelly. There was something a bit sad about him though, of course, Lisa couldn't allow herself to feel that now.

"I don't think Jeremy killed that woman the other night," Lisa said, her voice almost spiteful now.

"You think maybe I killed her?"

"Your hand, Sam."

"What about my hand?"

"It's shaking."

He looked down at his hand as if it belonged to somebody else. It was shaking. "So?"

"So I'm afraid the gun will misfire accidentally. I know you wouldn't mean to hurt me but —"

A knock on the door.

"Who is it?" Jenkins half shouted.

"Got a customer complaining about his bill, Mr. Jenkins."

"Can't you handle it, for Christ's sake?"

"He won't talk to nobody but you, Mr. Jenkins."

Under his breath, Jenkins muttered an especially filthy word. Lisa felt her cheeks burn. Among the many other things he was not, Sam Jenkins was no gentleman.

The gun went back into his holster. "You

better let things lie, Lisa. If you know what's good for you."

"You know Jeremy didn't kill that girl, don't you?"

Jenkins looked rattled and put-upon now. "You just leave me alone, Lisa. You get the hell out of here and you leave me alone."

Lisa could recall seeing Sam Jenkins when she was a little girl. In those days he was church people, trying to mount a show of respectability for the townspeople. But he soon gave up and gave in to his womanizing and alcoholic ways. Now to the respectable people of the community, he was a pariah and his hotel was looked upon as a real sin den.

"Go on, Lisa. Get out of here."

"Won't you help Jeremy, Sam? Can't you find the decency in your heart?"

Sam looked like a mother-lost beagle. "Go on, Lisa," Sam Jenkins said but there was no force in his words now. He sounded weary and old.

She came close to him, holding her breath because he still had the smell of the whore on him. "You're going to let him hang, Sam?"

He stared at her and shook his head. "I'm just doing what I need to to survive,

Lisa. Maybe respectable people like you can't understand that." There was a faint sense of anger in his words but mostly there was just the same weariness.

She thought of the envelope she'd tucked up her sleeve. Perhaps it was something that would help Jeremy.

Perhaps.

"Good-bye, Sam," Lisa said, brushing past him and out the door then past the pimple-faced young man who served as Sam Jenkins's assistant.

All she could think of now was the envelope and what it might hold.

Chapter Six

The ride to Arthur Hunt's massive ranch took twenty minutes from town.

From the livery Sam Jenkins got a bay gelding that the colored livery hand assured him was the fastest presently in stable.

The stage road was dusty in the mid-afternoon autumn sunlight. From an apple orchard sloping over a nearby hill, Jenkins could smell ripe and ready winesaps. He thought of apple pie with a tall glass of chill white milk standing next to it. He had no boyhood pleasure left in him, just the dour pleasures of his kind of middle age — rough whiskey and rougher women.

But however he tried to distract himself on his ride to Hunt's ranch, his mind always returned to the same thing: the presence of Lisa Tate in his room. What had she been looking for? Worse, what might she have found?

Only reluctantly had he become involved with Arthur Hunt's scheme to set up his own son for murder. Only reluctantly had he agreed to let Hunt come in and kill the girl and then bring the unconscious Jeremy, who'd been on a two-day bender, up the back stairs and put him in the same room as the dead girl.

He would never have agreed if he hadn't been into Arthur Hunt for poker. More than three thousand dollars. Art had promised to cancel the debt if Sam helped stage the murder. Of course, you wouldn't have expected your own cousin to hold you to the three-thousand-dollar debt in the first place. Much as he occasionally hated to admit it, Sam and Arthur Hunt were first cousins, their mothers having come to this state when it was still a territory. Of course, Arthur's mother had married better, much better in fact, and so Sam and his kin were always considered to be poor in-laws not only in wealth but in breeding and manners. Sometimes Arthur treated Sam the way no beast of burden should be treated. And Arthur was always reminding Sam about all the reasons Sam had to be grateful . . . including his help in getting Sam the manager's job at the run-down hotel he called home.

So now Arthur had gotten Sam involved in the ultimate misadventure . . . killing.

As he had asked himself over and over the past fifty-six hours, Sam wondered —

what kind of man would set up his own son for murder?

The aroma of winesaps soon gave way to the smells of cattle droppings and grass burned brown from the slanting autumn sun.

Jenkins passed beneath a fancy wooden arch that identified the ranch as THE LAZY 8 and then moved the gelding smartly past outbuildings that had recently been whitewashed and now dazzled in the sunlight and then past a bunkhouse that was really just a very long log cabin. Few white men were to be seen. They'd be out in the valleys and hills of the ranch. Chinese and red Indians were the only people Jenkins saw now.

The ranch house was built of wood and stone, a very fancy house for these parts, with a slanting roof of red tiles and trellises that lent the relatively new house a sense of age and permanence.

Jenkins tied the gelding to a hitching post and went up to the door. He was shown inside by a Chinese woman who spoke several sentences but not a word that Jenkins could understand. Still speaking unintelligibly, she showed Jenkins into a shaded den filled with leather and hardwood furnishings. One complete wall contained books. Another was filled with charts assessing various kinds of cattle, complete with detailed illustrations of each type.

Behind the wide, orderly desk sat a chunky man in a blue Western shirt. He was bald with fringes of white hair over his ears and had blunt features that gave him a crude kind of handsomeness. A black fountain pen was lost in a massive, sunburned hand that showed dozens of scars, nicks, and cuts. Art Hunt didn't look up. He only said, "I'd appreciate it if you'd sit down over there and be quiet till I finish with this requisition form. If you want a drink, there's some good brandy in the bottle by the picture of the governor there." Then he added, with relish and sarcasm, "Cousin."

At first, Jenkins had intended not to take up the offer of brandy. But as he sat there in the quiet, cool room, feeling the luxury and peacefulness of the place, he started thinking about Lisa Tate again. Why had she been in his room? What might she have found?

He went over and helped himself to the brandy. Decanter clinked against glass.

Still not looking up from his writing, Art Hunt said, "You've got some pretty bad shakes there, Sam. You'd better start taking things easy."

"We really need to talk, Art."

Art sighed. "You're just like a little kid, Sam. No patience. Now you sit there and be quiet and I'll be with you in a minute or two."

Hunt had still not looked up.

Sam Jenkins sat there and closed his eyes. The den smelled pleasantly of pipe smoke and furniture polish. Sipping brandy, he tried to imagine what it would be like to live in a house like this. Servants to wait on you. Comfortable furniture. Everything clean and tidy.

"Sam."

Sam opened his eyes, realized he'd been drifting off.

"I'm ready to talk now, Sam."

Jenkins set his drink down on the coffee table in front of him. "I found Lisa Tate in my hotel room this afternoon."

Art Hunt was not a man given to panic. Still, Jenkins could see the disturbing effect his words had had on the other man. Jenkins took some pleasure in that.

"You talked to her?"

"Yes," Jenkins said.

"What did she say?"

"She said she didn't think Jeremy really killed the girl."

Art Hunt said, "And where the hell did she get that idea?"

"I don't know, Art."

"You didn't get drunk and —"

"You seem to forget, Sam. I'm as much a part of this as you are, remember? You may have actually killed the girl but I helped set everything up."

Art Hunt waved off his words. "Did she find anything?"

"I don't know."

"Then she didn't say?"

"No."

"Did you ask?"

"Yes."

"You didn't search her or anything?"

"I was called downstairs."

"Fine."

"No need to be sarcastic, Art. I did what I could."

Art rubbed his wide hand across his bald pate. This was a nervous mannerism that for some reason had always irritated Sam Jenkins. Now, Art sighed. "I shouldn't have gotten so riled. Sorry."

"Maybe she didn't turn up anything."

"Maybe."

"Maybe she's just groping around in the dark."

"Maybe."

"Anyway, with Sheriff Larson laid up, she probably won't get real far. That was a good idea — shooting him."

Art Hunt leaned forward on the desk. Put together, his hands appeared to be the size of a large rock. "The idea was to scare him, not shoot him. He only got shot because somebody named Cage showed up and pushed him out of the way."

"You didn't want to shoot him?"

"You mean you haven't figured it out yet, Sam?"

"Figured what out yet?"

An unlikely grin came over Art Hunt's face. "You know, sometimes I swear our mothers made it up about you and me bein' cousins. You know that?"

"I still don't know what you're talking about."

Art Hunt leaned forward. "You remember when my wife Melissa died in that fire two years ago."

Sam shook his head. "A fire I know damn well you set."

Art Hunt waved his hand. "What I didn't know at the time was that she'd changed her will. The ranch, which was

65

hers to begin with, you remember, went to Jeremy and not me. But if something were to happen to Jeremy —"

"Damn," Sam said. "That's why you set him up."

"If he goes and gets himself hanged, cousin, then the ranch and all our holdings revert back to me."

"You're some cold sonofabitch, Art. You surely are that."

Art Hunt smiled. "Why, you sound downright envious, cousin." Then he quit smiling. "We're going to need Juanita over at the café."

"Why Juanita? What's she got to do with it?"

"She's going to carry a revolver in with dinner tonight."

"What?"

"That's right. And just about midnight, Jeremy's going to make a break for it and a deputy's going to kill him."

"A deputy? You mean Ron Sorenson."

"That's exactly who I mean, cousin. That's exactly who I mean."

Then Art Hunt sat back in his chair and stared at Sam and as usual Sam felt self-conscious, uncouth, unmannered, and stupid. You could just look at Art's hard bright eyes and tell that this man knew everything there was to know.

Then Art sniffed the air.

"God damn, cousin, you should wash yourself afterwards," Art said.

"Afterwards?"

"After you've been with a whore."

He sniffed the air again. "I can smell her clear across the room here."

Then he laid down his plans for Juanita at the café.

Chapter Seven

When she got back home, Lisa Tate heard her mother moaning from upstairs. For the past twenty years, Irene Tate had suffered from the most painful and debilitating kind of arthritis. She had visited a variety of doctors and a variety of clerics but none had been able to help her. For the past ten years, she had lain in her upstairs bed, photographs and mementos of her long-dead husband all around her and a little silver bell she tinkled when things got especially bad and she required the help of her daughter.

Lisa had planned to sit in the wing chair in the front room and examine the envelope she'd taken from Sam Jenkins's coat. But now there was no time for that.

Bringing foul-smelling liniment and two plump white marshmallows, she climbed the stairs, her steps echoing off the narrow walls leading to the upper floor. She had been climbing these stairs since she'd been a girl of six. While other children had played, or studied together in groups, or fallen in love, she'd been helping her mother. Only rarely had she resented the fact — and then she'd felt quite guilty. It was hardly her mother's fault that she was as sick as she was.

In the golden sunlight, the wallpaper of pink flowers with green stems made the upstairs hallway seem wider and brighter than usual. From two doors down came the moaning, accompanied by whispers and fragments of prayers. Sometimes the pain got so bad her mother was delirious and began to talk to various saints to whom she regularly prayed. Sometimes she even talked to her dead husband and asked him to take her wherever he was presently.

When Lisa peeked into her mother's room, she saw a tiny gray-haired woman in a wrinkled white robe whose bones and joints were so twisted she looked deformed. The arthritis would eventually claim most of her body, her doctors agreed.

"Good afternoon, Mother," Lisa said, entering the room and going over to the gray-haired woman with the faded blue eyes and the too-white lips. Waxen lips they were, the sort you saw worn in funeral homes by corpses.

Her mother muttered something resembling a hello.

The liniment went on first.

The stuff smelled strong as the rotgut whiskey poor men in these parts drank with dismaying frequency. You could almost see a mist rising from the bed. At first her mother continued to moan and to roll her eyes so that she seemed to be slipping into unconsciousness. But gradually, the moans softened; they didn't go away entirely but they did become less adamant in pitch and panic.

Now, the moans were no louder than purrs. Her mother patted her daughter's hand. "Thank you, honey."

"You're welcome, Mother."

"You're such a good girl."

Lisa patted her mother's hand. "Probably not as good as you think, Mother. At least not in my heart."

Her mother smiled. "Horrible things in your heart, Lisa?"

"Oh, you know, the usual things all human beings feel, I suppose. Too much pity for myself and not enough for others. And anger. And remorse. And a desire for vengeance."

"They haven't set him free yet?"

"Not yet."

"You wait and see. They will."

"I don't think so, Mother. I really don't.

People in these parts have been looking for a way to pay back Arthur Hunt for years. Now they've found a way."

"But you said you're sure he's innocent."

"I know he is, Mother. I'm sure of it. But that doesn't mean that anybody else is sure of it. Not the sheriff. Not the judge."

Even this brief a conversation had worn her mother out. The old woman lay her narrow head back on a vast white pillow. Above her head, on the wall, was a crucifix. Behind the crucifix was a long switch of palm from the previous Palm Sunday.

Without raising her head, her mother took Lisa's hands. "Why don't we close our eyes and pray for Jeremy?"

Lisa sighed. Much as she believed in God, sometimes all her mother's praying got Lisa down. There, she already felt guilty for having such a thought.

"All right, Mother, let's pray. And then I'll give you your marshmallows."

"Are they big ones?"

"Very big ones."

"And chewy?"

"Very chewy."

"And sweet?"

"Very sweet."

Her mother laughed softly. "See, I sound just like you did when you were a little girl."

Lisa laughed, too, and put her face against her mother's. "Oh, I love you so much. All your suffering and you can still joke."

She could not help the tears in her eyes.

When she knew that her mother was asleep, Lisa went downstairs, freshened up, had a cup of tea and half a biscuit, then went into the front room and sat down to have a look at the envelope she'd taken from Sam Jenkins's coat pocket.

At first, the envelope appeared to be quite normal. A plain white number ten envelope such as any reputable business would use in its offices. She slit the envelope with her nail and looked inside.

She was so disappointed, she tore the envelope into four strips and tossed them to the floor. The envelope had held nothing. She felt exhausted. She had not slept well since Jeremy had been arrested. During this time, almost in a sympathetic response, her mother's arthritis had seemed to worsen.

Now the envelope, the one thing she'd been able to take from Sam's room, had proved useless.

No help to Jeremy.

No help to Jeremy at all.

This time, she did cry, exhausted tears that spoke of anger rather than sorrow.

No help at all.

Chapter Eight

"They'll come tonight," Ron Sorenson said. "Art and his men."

Cage and Sorenson stood at the barred window in the front room of the sheriff's office and looked out at the dusty street.

"Probably come from the west, right up the street there, and then surround the building here and come in and demand him."

"How many men, do you figure?"

"I'm told he's hired half a dozen toughs and that they're out there at the ranch with him."

Cage sighed and turned away from the window. "Whatever happened to that new life I was going to lead?"

"Beg pardon?"

"Oh, nothing," Cage said, heading for the coffeepot.

The deputy came back and picked up a carbine, checked it over. "If we can just hang on till morning."

"The train isn't going to do us any good if we can't get Jeremy on it."

"There'll be federal troops on the train. There usually are, anyway, from the fort. I figure one of us can enlist them in our little enterprise. Not even Art Hunt would go up against federal troops."

"To save his son?"

The deputy scratched his head. "That's the funny thing."

"What is?"

"Art and Jeremy've never gotten along much."

"Really?"

"Nope. Fact is, most people around here always considered Jeremy kind of a mama's boy. Tied pretty tight to his mama's apron strings."

"What happened to his mama?"

"Died awhile back. Fire."

Cage stared at him. Something about the statement made him curious. "Fire on the ranch?"

"Yup."

"But it didn't hurt Art?"

"Nope."

"Sheriff Larson look into that?"

"Pretty much. I guess you could say he had some suspicions but he couldn't prove them."

Cage went over and sat in Larson's chair. Despite the fact that the wheels on the legs squeaked as they were moved around, it was a damn fine chair.

The deputy dropped into a chair across from him.

"Hunt stand to gain anything from his wife's death?"

"She was the one with the money."

"Oh?"

"Kind of a mousy little woman all her life. Sweet-natured but fragile. Daughter of a rich man from the East who came out here to make it big in cattle. She inherited the ranch from her father. Then here comes young Art Hunt. Strapping fellow and handsome and all that. He just sort of took over her life. It was almost sickening to see how much that little woman loved Art. And he always kept women on the side in town here. One especially named Belle."

"So Art Hunt had nothing till he married his wife and then he had everything?"

"Correct. But to be honest, I've got to say he's worked that ranch real hard and turned it into something a lot bigger than even her father could have."

"Know anything about this Belle?"

"Prostitute. Very beautiful. Very hard. She's been here twenty years, which would about put her in her mid-thirties. She probably knows everything there is to know about Hunt."

"You know where she lives?"

"Sure. In a suite in the Windsor Hotel."

"So I could go over there and see her if I had a mind to?"

"If you had a mind to."

Cage looked up at the clock. "Maybe I'll do that in a little while. You be all right here alone?"

"Sure. Long as it stays daylight. Hunt won't make any moves during the day."

Cage stood up, nodded to the gun cabinet. "Guess it's about time."

"Time?"

"For me to strap on guns."

"Oh. Yeah."

"Been a while." Cage smiled without humor. "And I'd had hopes that it would be a long time before I'd have to again."

The deputy stood up now, too. "I know you don't like bein' here, Cage. But if you weren't —" The deputy shook his head solemnly.

Cage cuffed him on the bicep then went over to the gun cabinet. He found two .44s and strapped them on. They felt heavy and uncomfortable after four months of being a plain city man with no association with the law, a man who could walk down the street without carrying a weapon.

Cage fixed his hat at a more comfortable angle and said, "I'll be over at the Windsor Hotel."

"Sure thing," the deputy said then grinned. "Sheriff."

Chapter Nine

Just as Cage was departing for the Windsor Hotel, Sam Jenkins rode back into town. He took his mount directly to the livery, where he placed it in the care of an elderly black man Sam had long considered too outspoken for a man of such dark skin.

At this time of the afternoon, the streets were crowded. Many farm wives came into town on such a pleasant afternoon, beginning the long process of stocking up for the harsh realities of winter. There had been a time when Sam would have stood on one of the street corners, pretending to be waiting for somebody, and ogled all the passing women. But no more. Whenever his groin ached with the need for release, he just found himself a whore. It was much easier.

But now there wasn't even time for a whore. Art Hunt's orders still rang in his ears, the way Art's orders always did, like the words of a scolding parent.

Convince her, Sam.

You're good at convincing people.

Convince her, Sam.

Or else.

In five minutes, Sam stood outside the Bluebird Café. Juanita got a break about this time every day. Usually she went out back and rolled herself a cigarette and sat there smoking, fanning herself with her apron to cool the sweat she'd worked up in the hot little kitchen where she was the cook. Juanita wasn't much to look at maybe but she had wondrous full breasts and a bountiful smile that not even her bad need of dental work could ruin.

Sam went around back.

Instead of being alone, Juanita sat on one barrel and a young punk with fancy cowboy clothes sat on another. The punk had obviously looked past Juanita's lack of beauty and found her real charms.

Juanita's graying hair was worn back in a loose bun today. Her clothes consisted of a drab gray cotton dress that was sweat-stained in the armpits. Only recently had her face begun to look worn, the way a frontier woman's did as she reached thirty or so.

She looked surprised to see Sam. "What're you doing here, Sam?"

"Need to talk to you," Sam said, glaring at the punk who was glaring right back.

"Kinda busy, Sam," she said, and flicked her eyes to the punk.

"Tell sonny boy here to go take a walk."

"Sonny boy?" the punk said, and started to stand up.

"Better stop him," Sam said.

Juanita was sensible enough to grab the punk's arm. "He maybe don't look like much, Eddy, but I seen him break a man's face with one punch."

"This old bastard?" the young punk said.

Sam hit him. Hit him so hard the young punk fell straight down to the ground, covered his face with his hands, red blood seeping from between his fingers, and cried.

Sam, still enraged, went over and kicked the young punk in the ribs.

"Now you get up and get out of here," Sam said. "Or I'll hurt you even worse."

Between his hands, and between sobs, the young punk said something — more likely cursing Sam — but Sam no longer cared. His anger was gone, the way his desire for a woman was gone once his loins had taken care of their necessary business.

In an almost fatherly way, Sam said,

81

"Now you get up and get the hell out of here. You understand me?"

The young punk muttered more curses and started the humiliating struggle to his feet.

Juanita got off the barrel and knelt next to the young punk, taking him fondly under the arm and helping him to his feet.

The young punk was pretty shaky. The dark red blood was coming faster now. From her apron Juanita took a plain white rag and applied it to the young punk's nose. He would never again be quite so pretty as he had been only a few minutes earlier.

The young punk glared at Sam.

Juanita nudged him gently on his way.

"You had no call to do that, Sam," Juanita said, obviously for the benefit of the young punk, who was just now disappearing around the corner.

Soon as he was out of sight, Juanita burst into hearty laughter. "Sam, that's some goddamn temper you've got, you know that? And it's all the worse for you lookin' like this real mild man. Sure does catch them young 'uns by surprise."

Sam, all business now, took a Navy Colt from inside his suitcoat and handed it over to Juanita.

"What's this?" she said. "I don't want no gun."

"Isn't for you. It's for Jeremy Hunt."

"Jeremy Hunt?"

"Yes," Sam said, sitting her down on the edge of the barrel again. "And you're going to take it to him."

Chapter Ten

As soon as she heard the moan, Lisa rushed to the top of the stairs to see if her mother was all right. When she peeked into the bedroom, she found the woman rolled over on her side, sleeping. Occasionally, even in her sleep, her mother moaned.

Lisa bent down and kissed her sweat-slicked gray hair then went back downstairs to tidy up the house.

A clock had begun to tick in Lisa's mind with the unceasing urgency of a metronome. A clock that said that in the morning, less than seventeen hours away now, Jeremy would be taken away from her.

Forever.

She had to do something.

Anything.

But what?

Hoping that cleaning the house would distract her momentarily from her misery, Lisa picked up the feather duster and went to work.

She had never before let the house get too cluttered or dusty, but since the hour

Jeremy had been arrested, Lisa had paid the house no heed at all.

Now everything was coated with a fine film of dust.

She was just about to work on the windowsills when she saw on the carpet the envelope she'd torn up.

Bending to pick up the envelope, she took the four tattered parts and started to stick them in her pocket. Which was when she noticed the handwriting on the inside flap of the envelope, handwriting she hadn't noticed before.

The penciled scribbling read:

Sally Dane — $200

Lisa felt as if a great blow had just made her entire body weak. She slipped to the edge of the closest chair and read and re-read the writing.

Sally Dane.

$200.

There were two pieces of significant news here.

The first was that Sally Dane's name and a dollar amount were found on the envelope Lisa had taken from Sam Jenkins's coat pocket.

The other was the name "Sally Dane" itself. She was the woman whom Jeremy had supposedly killed.

What had Sally Dane done for Sam Jenkins that was worth $200?

Lisa stood up, undoing the strings of her apron and setting down her feather duster.

She still felt unreal and overly excited. She had been waiting for more than two days for something like this. She had to act on it quickly.

The trouble was — how? Sheriff John T. Larson was laid up with a gunshot wound and much as she liked and felt sorry for Ron Sorenson, Larson's deputy, he would not know what to do with this piece of information.

Hurrying to the closet, she took down a white shawl, wrapped it around her shoulders, and went out the front door.

She was not quite sure where she was going.

All she knew for sure was that she was going to get Jeremy Hunt out of jail — one way or the other.

"What if I get caught, Sam?"

"You won't get caught."

"If I did get caught, I'd tell who put me up to it."

"You're not going to get caught, I tell you."

"You wouldn't give a damn anyway,

would you, if I spent the rest of my life rotting in some jail cell?"

Sam Jenkins sighed. Despite the slight chill of the afternoon, the autumn sun was hot when you sat out in it for a time. They were still in the alley behind the restaurant where Juanita was a cook, still sitting on barrels.

He'd been trying to reason with Juanita for nearly fifteen minutes now.

"You know what's going to happen, don't you, Sam?"

"What?"

"He's going to take this gun I bring in to him, Jeremy is, and he's going to shoot somebody. And then somebody's going to shoot him."

"It won't happen that way."

"Then where will Art be?"

"Huh?"

"The whole idea behind me bringing Jeremy the gun is so he'll go free, right?"

"Right."

"But if Ron Sorenson shoots him while he's escaping, what's the point? Art wants Jeremy alive because he loves him so much."

Oh yeah, he loves him so much, Sam thought. *He loves him so much, he killed his mother and framed him for murder. And now he's going to see to it that he gets killed.*

"Ain't that right?" Juanita said.

"That's right, Juanita," Sam said. "Except it won't happen that way."

"It won't?"

"Nope. I'll make sure a horse is waiting for Jeremy. By the time the deputy figures out what's happened, Jeremy will be long gone."

"How about that new man they took off the train to be sheriff?"

"He won't bother nothin' any more than the deputy will."

Juanita looked at him. "How much I get?"

"Hundred and fifty."

"She was a friend of mine, you know. Sally Dane."

"I know."

"And somebody killed her, whether it was Jeremy or not."

"He was liquored up. He didn't know what he was doin'."

"I still don't like to help him, though. Not the way he cut her up. She was a pretty gal."

"A hundred and fifty dollars, Juanita. You just set your thinkin' cap on that for a while. Think of everything you could buy with it."

She tossed a rock at a small, rib-sharp mongrel dog that was stalking the alley for food. "Git," she said.

"New chiffon dress."

"Well," she said.

"New picture hat with one of them big bows in back."

"Well," she said.

"New garter with one of them little fake diamonds in it."

"Well," she said.

"You'd sure look pretty in a garter like that."

"My legs ain't what they used to be."

"Garter'd set 'em off real nice, even if they aren't what they used to be."

"I jus' keep thinkin'."

"About what?"

"You know."

"No I don't."

" 'Bout how he cut her up and all. Jeremy, I mean."

"He was liquored up, hon. That's all. He wouldn't do nothing like that sober. He's just a kid."

She sighed. "I suppose."

He said, "Nice new bolero like you like so much."

"Well."

"Nice new linen cuffs."

"Well."

"Nice new —"

"Aw, hell, Sam Jenkins, you knew I was gonna do it anyways."

This time her rock hit the little dog right on the side of the head. "Little pecker," she said. Then threw another rock at him.

Chapter Eleven

The Windsor Hotel tried awfully hard to be grand but didn't quite make it. Instead of real gilt, the trim was carved wood painted in a runny gold color. Instead of gargoyles guarding either side of the wide entrance door, there were two ugly, squatting little figures that more resembled lap dogs. Instead of genuine Persian rugs in the wide lobby area, there were small braided throw rugs that had been dyed to resemble Persians. They only managed to look blotchy.

The man on duty behind the desk wore a celluloid collar stained with blood from shaving and sweat from working. He was a fleshy Irishman with thinning red hair and rheumy eyes from too close an acquaintance with the bottle.

"I'd like to see Belle."

The clerk could not take his eyes off Cage's badge. "Never saw you before."

"I'm just helping out."

"I heard John T. got shot."

"Right."

"Also heard it was the fault of the acting sheriff."

Despite himself, Cage felt his cheeks turn hot and red. So John T. had wasted no time in telling his story to people.

"I guess that's open to interpretation."

"She ain't up anyway."

"Beg pardon."

"Belle. She ain't up yet."

Cage raised his eyes to the big Ingram behind the desk. "It's getting on evening."

"Never bothers Belle none. She likes to play all night and sleep all day."

"Get her up for me."

The Irishman grinned. "If you think she's gonna be impressed with your badge, you're wrong."

Cage was serious. "Get her."

In all, it took twenty minutes.

While he waited, Cage sat in a chair so deep and soft it threatened to swallow him up. During this time, he rolled himself two cigarettes and thought a great deal about where he'd be if he'd stayed on that train and hadn't ventured out into Willow Creek for breakfast.

Oh, yes; and he fumed over the story that John T. Larson was spreading.

Cage's fault indeed.

Why that old bastard —

"She ain't happy."

Cage looked up from his thoughts to see the Irishman standing over him.

"She ain't happy," the Irishman repeated. "She said she was dreaming some very nice dreams when I started banging on her door."

"I can go up?"

The Irishman grinned. "I'd sure take a gun along. You don't know what Belle's like when she's mad."

Cage struggled up from the chair. "Thanks for your help."

The Irishman nodded then grinned again. "Sure wish I could be there to see it. Sure like to see Belle cut lawmen down to size."

Belle lived on the third floor at the end of a long hall. The door was open a crack. Cage pushed in.

The first thing that hit him was a dinner plate. It smashed over his shoulder.

The second thing that hit him was a wineglass. It exploded like a rifle blast two inches from his head.

A buxom woman five years past her prime was doing the throwing. She sat in the center of an elegant settee in a sheer, floor-length robe that was trimmed in dark fur.

The third thing she threw was a butcher knife that came so close to Cage's rib cage, he had to jump away.

The knife, thrumming, stuck deep in the wooden trim around the door.

"There," she said in a voice rich with years of whiskey and tobacco. "Now that I've got that out of my system, you can come in and sit down."

The room was more like a small apartment and it was an oasis of good taste in this cheapjack hotel. The furnishings looked Eastern-made, the decoration done with taste and style. Belle was like that herself. Despite her age, her regal face — she had the imperious outsize features of royalty — still showed great beauty, especially the dark gaze, which was both intelligent and ironic. Her body was outsize, too — deep cleavage and generous, silken hips that tapered down to slender legs and surprisingly little feet, the toenails of which were painted a soft aqua color that would have looked garish on anybody else.

"So you're the man who almost got John T. killed," she said.

This time, his face didn't turn crimson. He merely ground his teeth. "So I've heard."

She laughed. "Too bad you didn't get

him killed while you were at it."

"You've got something against our beloved sheriff?"

She picked up the irony in his tone and seemed grateful for it, as if he'd handed her a gift. "You like him a lot, too?"

"He's all right, I suppose. A little larger-than-life for my taste."

She laughed. "What I hate is his hypocrisy. Every time he thinks the city council's getting fed up with him, he decides to close down all the whorehouses. Now, personally, I haven't worked in the houses in years but I feel sorry for the girls who're still there. They don't get paid much as it is. And to have John T. come in pretending he's a Bible-thumper —" She shook her head. "The worst part is the hypocrisy, though. During one of his raids — he fanned his men throughout the house — he took some little frightened girl and made her get in the closet with him. I'll spare your tender ears the details but suffice it to say John T. took his pleasure — right in the middle of a raid."

Cage decided to get to the reason he'd come here. "I'm told John T. and Arthur Hunt don't get along."

At the mention of Hunt's name, Cage sensed a shift in the woman's attitude.

The playfulness was gone. She was now guarded, even a little apprehensive.

"I don't talk about Art," she said softly. "Not to anybody."

"I'm the acting sheriff, ma'am. I'm afraid you've got to talk to me."

Some of the merriment returned to her eyes but only briefly. "You think anybody who throws dishes the way I do is afraid of the law?"

He smiled. "We shouldn't have any problems, you and I."

"Oh, boy."

"Beg pardon?"

"You're going to try and be my 'friend,' aren't you?"

His cheeks started to become hot again.

"Don't try that tack with me, kid. I've been places and seen things that make you look like a real tinhorn to me. No offense intended in that last remark, by the way. I'm just telling you the truth. But just don't waste your time pretending that you and I have got a lot of things in common because we don't. If you want to ask questions, ask away. But spare me the psychology."

"Did Art Hunt murder his wife?"

A bitter laugh sounded in her throat. "You don't waste time, do you?"

"You said to ask away."

"I really don't want to talk about Art. That's been over for some time now."

"How long?"

"Long enough."

"Years?"

"I suppose."

"How many years?"

"Why's it so blamed important?"

"Because I want to know if you were friends with him during the time he was planning the death of his wife."

"A while ago you were asking me *if* he killed his wife. Now you're telling me he did."

"From what I understand, it's a strong possibility."

"John T. hates Art. That's why he spread that rumor."

"Were you still seeing Hunt during that time?"

"I suppose."

"Did he ever talk about his plans?"

For the first time, she averted her eyes. "As I told you, I don't talk about Art."

Cage, tired of sitting, got up and crossed the elegantly appointed room. He went to the shutters, opened one side of them, and looked down into the street. Nearing supper-time now, the traffic was thinning some.

"How about his son?" Cage said.

"Jeremy?"

"Yes."

"What about him?"

"How does Hunt get along with his son?"

"How does any man get along with his son?"

"Meaning what?" Cage closed the shutters and walked back to the chair across from the settee. He rolled himself a cigarette.

She shrugged. "Meaning fathers and sons always have troubles."

"What kind of troubles?"

"Have you met Jeremy?"

"Yes. Why?"

"Well, he's hardly the kind of strapping, fearless son a man like Art would want to have."

"He seemed fine to me."

"He took after his mother too much for Art's taste. And the girl didn't help."

"Girl?"

"Jeremy's ladyfriend. A local teacher named Lisa Tate. One of those uppity girls who thinks she's better than a lot of other people." She laughed again. This time the sound was nasty. "She's been giving him piano lessons. You should have heard Art when he found out about that."

"Doesn't sound as if Art gives much

of a damn about his son."

"Like I said, fathers and sons always have problems."

"Yes, but this seems to go beyond 'father and son' problems. Way beyond." He paused. "I'm told Art married his wife for her money."

"That's an old story."

"But a true one?"

"Maybe. But he improved everything he touched."

"Did he improve you?"

"I don't care much for your sense of humor."

"I'm just trying to figure you out."

"I've been trying to do that for years. And I finally gave up."

"You seem loyal to Hunt but you don't seem to like him much. Does he have a new woman?"

"You sure aren't subtle, are you?"

"There isn't time to be subtle."

She sighed, then looked at her surprisingly delicate hands lying now in her lap. "I guess."

"You guess he has a new woman?"

She put her head down and whispered, "Yes."

"A young woman?"

She nodded.

She startled him by starting to cry. Moments earlier, he would not have believed she was capable of tears.

"I guess I'm getting old," she said, tears making her words indistinct.

"There's no reason you have to be loyal to him," Cage said quietly in the silence of her grief.

"Yes, there is."

"Why?"

She raised her gaze to meet his. "Because I still love him."

Cage sighed. "I'm sorry." Then, "Do you think he wanted to get rid of Jeremy the same way he got rid of his wife?"

"You don't give up, do you?"

"It's not my job to give up."

"I wish you'd leave."

"Jeremy's life is at stake."

"I never cared for Jeremy."

Cage shook his head. "You think Hunt would be this loyal to you?"

"I suppose not."

For a hopeful moment, Belle looked as if she were going to start talking again, maybe even saying things that would help Cage figure out what was going on in this town — but then he watched her as she withdrew into herself. "You go on now. You get out of here."

"But —"

She put her face into her hands and started sobbing.

Cage knew it was no use.

He left.

Chapter Twelve

The lawyer's name was William Dunhurst, or William Dunhurst, *Esquire,* as the fancy sign on the pebbled glass door leading to his office read.

But now Dunhurst, a stout and hale man in his mid-fifties, was not in his office.

No, he stood in the cell block in the rear of the sheriff's office and it was easy to see from the way his nostrils sniffed the air and the way his right eyebrow was cocked that William Dunhurst, Esquire, was not at all happy with where he found young Jeremy Hunt residing these days.

Jeremy watched the man walk down the aisle between the cells, a vain man in a three-piece suit with a large golden watch chain draped across his widening girth and a smart walking stick leading the way.

Except for Jeremy, the cell block was empty.

Jeremy had awakened only ten minutes earlier, having fallen into one of his frequent and troubled sleeps. Ever since waking up in that strange hotel room and being told that he had savagely murdered a young woman — ever since then, Jeremy had found that sleep was his only true friend.

"Afternoon, Jeremy," Dunhurst said, touching a wide hand delicately to his silver hair.

"Afternoon."

"Your father sent me."

"I see."

Dunhurst cocked his eyebrow again. "This isn't any time for your usual sarcasm. Your father would have been here himself except he's busy."

"Busy."

Dunhurst elected to ignore this second example of sarcasm. "He wanted to know if you needed anything."

"Yes. I need a key to this door and a fast horse." Miserably, Jeremy put his hands on the bars and tugged, as if wishing himself strength enough to pull the bars down. "Does he believe me yet?"

Dunhurst evaded Jeremy's gaze. "I told him what you said."

"He still thinks I killed her?"

"He takes you at your word."

"Oh, isn't that nice of him? Isn't that generous? He takes his son at his word."

Dunhurst frowned. "Maybe your father

hasn't been an ideal parent, Jeremy, but you've hardly been an ideal son either."

"So you're going to start this again?"

Dunhurst, perhaps because he received his considerable pay from Jeremy's father, was always quick to remind Jeremy that he was less than wonderful. Like Arthur Hunt, Dunhurst had always been disapproving of Jeremy. Not tough enough. Not interested enough in the things real boys were interested in. Moody. Sullen. Given much too young to drinking and carousing and getting into various minor skirmishes that caused his father abiding shame. And after the death of the boy's mother, things got only worse.

"They're still taking me out in the morning?"

"That is the plan, yes," Dunhurst said.

Jeremy pulled on the bars again. "That jury is going to convict me and you know it."

"A lot of things can happen between now and then," Dunhurst said with loud but empty zeal.

"I didn't kill her, Bill."

"All right."

" 'All right' isn't the same as saying 'I know you didn't.' "

"If you say you didn't, that's good enough for me, Jeremy."

Jeremy went back and sat on the edge of his bunk and put his face in his hands.

He had seen a hanging once — his father had taken him to it — and to the eyes of a ten-year-old it had been unbelievably savage. The way the man had cried and pleaded for them not to do it; the grim faces of the lawmen; the hooded visage of the hangman himself. And then the trapdoor falling open and the rope snapping the man's neck and the man's feet dangling. And then the quick loud celebration afterward, guns being fired into the air, and crowds of men heading to the saloon. . . .

"I know I couldn't have done it," Jeremy said, trying for the thousandth time to recall exactly what had happened that night in the hotel room. "I'd have some memory of it, Bill. Some kind of memory."

"Probably so."

A long silence ensued.

Dunhurst said, glancing around for fear of being overheard, "You're going to get a surprise with your meal tonight."

As if he hadn't heard, Jeremy kept his hands in his face.

"Did you hear me?" Dunhurst said.

Jeremy looked up. Shrugged. "A surprise? What're you talking about?"

Dunhurst glanced around again. "Not so loud."

Now Jeremy stood up again and came back to the bars. "What're you saying, Bill?"

"Just wait and see. That's what I'm saying."

"You mean —"

Dunhurst *shusshed* him. "You just wait till tonight. Then you act accordingly. Understand?"

Jeremy nodded.

Dunhurst stared at the younger man. "Your father wants you to know that he's thinking of you. That's why he's making sure you're getting your surprise."

"You tell him thank you," Jeremy said, feeling an almost exultant sense of gratitude, something he'd rarely felt for his father.

"Meanwhile, you just lie back there and get some sleep and wait for Juanita to bring your dinner over. You get me?"

"I get you."

"Just relax."

"Yes."

"And rest."

"Yes."

"Because you'll need your strength tonight."

Jeremy couldn't keep himself from

smiling. He was like an eight-year-old who'd just been given a Christmas gift in July.

Stout William Dunhurst nodded to Jeremy and then started to leave. At the cell block door, he turned around and said, "You just remember that your father's thinking of you."

Then he left.

Chapter Thirteen

Deputy Ron Sorenson was trying to break himself of the habit, but so far he hadn't had much luck. Maybe if he could get rid of the first habit he could then get rid of the second — which was drinking on the job.

Twice a day, once in the morning and once in the afternoon, he took out the photograph of David, the son he'd seen trampled by a horse right out here on Main Street.

Twice a day, he set the photograph on his desk and studied it with an intensity and melancholy that always caused him to shudder. And occasionally break into tears.

At these times, the deputy always thought of what might have been — and what had been, the horse rearing up and coming down on the little blond boy who'd wandered away from his father, the little boy screaming for help and trying to get out of the way, but the big sleek bay coming down with the force of the entire universe behind it, hooves flashing, whinnying in a fear just as instinctive as the boy's had been.

Then those terrible long minutes when the deputy had held his little boy in his arms right there in the middle of the street, men calling for a doc and women wailing, capable of no thought but of the boy whose name he kept calling again and again.

David.

Please David.

Please Lord.

David.

And then knowing, even before the doc finally arrived rumpled as always, knowing that David was dead.

Hail Mary full of.

(Not wanting to say what she was full of.)

And Our Father who aren't in heaven.

David.

Dead.

He never prayed again, the deputy didn't. When his wife tried to get him to pray with her one night, he slapped her with a viciousness that stunned them both.

Don't talk to me about no God.

(Our Father who aren't in heaven.)

But he never gave up the photograph.

When the snows came and it was time for the boy's birthday, or would have been anyway, he slept with the photograph in his hand, clutching it so tightly he sometimes bent it.

He had slept with the photograph through ten such birthdays now.

The boy David was deader than ever.

But the pain was alive in the deputy.

Fully alive.

"You all right?" Cage said.

"Whu?" the deputy said, dropping his feet from the desk to the floor. "What say?"

Cage studied him carefully. Two quick impressions. He'd been nipping, the deputy had, and you could smell it raw on the air; and he'd been crying. No doubt about that.

"I asked if you were all right."

"I'm fine."

"We've got a long night ahead of us."

The deputy sat up straight and wiped the tears from his eyes with the back of his hand. "You get anywhere with Belle?"

Cage hated himself for staring. He couldn't help it. You just didn't see a man cry that often. Especially this time of day. Then he saw the photograph turned facedown on the desk. He wondered what it showed.

"Seems she's still loyal to Arthur Hunt

even though he's got himself a new woman. Younger."

"I heard that. You want some coffee?"

"Thanks."

The deputy was shaky going over to the coffeepot. You couldn't tell if it was from grief or liquor. Cage wasn't sure which would be worse, given the long night ahead of them.

"Here you go," the deputy said, bringing Cage back a cup.

Cage looked at him straight on. "Maybe we'd better talk a little."

"Thought I'd go down the street and have some supper."

"You don't eat at home."

He shrugged. "The old woman and I don't get on so well these days."

"I see." Cage nodded to the deputy's cup. "Have a couple more of those when you're down there."

"Just because I'm drinking a bit doesn't mean I'm drunk."

"I know."

The deputy offered the most sorrowful smile Cage had ever seen. "But I'll drink three cups of the hottest, blackest coffee I can find. That suit you?"

"That'd suit me fine."

The deputy drained his coffee and

walked heavily to the door.

Just as he opened it, Lisa Tate appeared, lovely face tinted red from the cold of the late autumn afternoon. "Hello, Ron," she said.

"Afternoon, Miss Tate."

She looked in through the door and said, "Is this Mr. Cage?"

"One and the same," the deputy said.

"Think I could talk to him?"

The deputy glanced back at Cage. "Oh, I expect he might let you talk to him."

"Thanks, Ron. Say hello to your wife."

The deputy's face tightened. He nodded and walked out into the dusk.

Lisa came in and closed the door.

Chapter Fourteen

"Sally Dane? Is that somebody I should know?"

"She's the girl Jeremy allegedly killed."

"I see. I'm afraid I —"

"No need to apologize, Mr. Cage. You're only filling in. I shouldn't have been so short with you."

They sat in the front office, Cage with a cup of coffee, Lisa Tate with her hands in her lap. Every half minute or so she stared at the heavy door leading to the cell block.

They had been talking for fifteen minutes now and Cage still wasn't sure where the conversation was going.

"Do you know much about Sally Dane?" Cage asked.

"Not really. She was a prostitute who worked at various houses in town here."

"Did Jeremy know her before the killing?"

"Are you asking me if he slept with her?"

Cage shrugged. "I suppose. If that doesn't offend you."

"I don't have any illusions about Jeremy. He's hardly an angel."

"That doesn't answer my questions about Sally Dane."

She hesitated. "Yes, I suppose he did sleep with her."

"Then she wouldn't be shy about coming up to his room?"

"I thought you told me you were going to listen to this with an open mind."

"I am, Miss Tate. I'm just pointing out that if he knew her, then —"

"If he knew her, then he killed her?"

Cage sighed. "Look, Miss Tate. I'll admit that the case is confusing. So much so that I don't discount your theory that Jeremy's father set the whole thing up." He lowered his voice. "But there's something else you need to consider."

"What's that?"

"That he killed her."

"No." She shook her head. "No, that didn't happen."

"I'm afraid it may have, Miss Tate. He's known for drinking too much and for having a violent temper. To make things worse, he can't even remember most of the night. He was so drunk he had to take a room here in town rather than ride back to his father's ranch." He stared at her levelly. "He could have killed her, Miss Tate."

She dropped her chin to her neck. Shook

her head again. She put a slender hand to her breast. She looked like a young girl suddenly and Cage was moved. "I would know it here, in my heart, if he'd killed Sally Dane."

"All right."

"You don't have to humor me either, Mr. Cage. I'm speaking the truth."

Cage said nothing.

"Sally Dane has a sister here in town. A very angry girl named Gretta. Maybe you could go talk to her."

"I suppose I could."

"Ask her about the two hundred dollars. What it was for." She explained the figure that she'd found written in the envelope.

"All right, Miss Tate."

She looked up again. "He's innocent, Mr. Cage. Jeremy, I mean."

"I hope you're right. For your sake."

She smiled. "You still don't believe me, do you?"

"It isn't my job to believe or disbelieve, Miss Tate. All I care about is that Jeremy Hunt doesn't escape or get sprung from here."

Lisa Tate stood up. "May I see Jeremy now?"

Cage nodded. "Of course."

He opened the cell block door for her.

Chapter Fifteen

Arthur Hunt sat back in the leather chair behind his desk, sipping from the shot glass he'd just filled with sour mash whiskey.

He felt old and fatigued sometimes, memories rushing back as vivid as when they'd first taken place. . . .

Two years after Jeremy had been born, Arthur Hunt tried to drown him one day at the creek. Father and son were alone on the hot overcast day and even now Arthur Hunt would not have been able to tell you what came over him that day. Just — something.

Jeremy had been crawling along the edge of the creek, and Arthur — sitting up on the slope and checking his bay's shoes for pebbles, had been keeping a vague eye out for milk snakes. Snakes were the things his wife worried most about. In her mind, snakes were everywhere, just waiting to snap at her son.

He supposed, when he thought about it later, that it was because of the will. He'd always sensed that Jeremy would somehow wrest the ranch from him — just as he had, his mother changing the will at the last. There could be no other possible explanation. Here he'd married a plump plain woman and endured years of her father's abuse and outrage and all for what — so he would have to split the ranch with a son he hadn't wanted in the first place?

So he'd come down the slope and there was little Jeremy waddling around — he'd been a tub of an infant — and then Arthur Hunt couldn't stop himself.

He seized up the boy as if offering a sacrifice to unseen gods and then plunged him deep into the muddy creek water.

The boy's little pink hands grasped uselessly at the air and every few moments you could see his tiny blond head trying to jerk its way out of the water.

Arthur did not let up.

"You little sonofabitch," he said, and plunged the boy deeper.

And then an image of his wife filled Arthur's mind.

"How could you let him drown? How could you?"

And there would be months of wailing and tears.

And finally, even though she could never prove anything, there might be suspicion.

And Arthur knew well how suspicion worked.

How you think no, he couldn't have done something like that.

But then you keep thinking.

Thinking.

And then you say yes, yes, he's exactly the kind of bastard who could do something like that.

And so even if he didn't do it — even if it could never be proved in a half-dozen centuries — you've got this person tried and convicted in your own mind.

And somebody you've tried and convicted —

Well, you're sure as hell not going to leave somebody like that the biggest spread this side of Yuma now, are you?

Not by a long shot.

When he yanked his son from the water, Jeremy's face was a deep blue.

And the kid was puking up so much he couldn't even cry out.

He flung the kid in the long grass and started to pump the water out of his lungs.

O sweet Jesus, please don't let him die.

Please don't let him die.

I made a mistake, don't you understand, I made a mistake.

And Jeremy did not die, of course, that

day there on the long grass slope.

No, he lived to become his mother's true love, the only human being on which she'd ever doted. Where Art was concerned, she'd given up on doting, letting him have his women and his ways. If she did mind, she never said so anyway.

She didn't even protest when he went on long hunting trips with his friends across the border and ended up in a certain much-celebrated whorehouse outside Mexico City.

She did not even seem to mind when the church ladies began whispering how Art stayed nights with Belle and how the two were seen kissing romantic as young fools on the moon-silvered backporch of the three-story house she ran in those days.

The night he killed her, he thought of all these things. There had been great rage in her killing — knocking her unconscious, spreading kerosene over "her" wing of the house — and that had surprised him. Though he had never loved her, still he'd always felt spurned by her. Though he'd never desired her, still he'd felt coldly shut out of her bed when he could not make her juices flow. He had listened to her final screams, the sound lurid as the flames against the night, there in the darkness muttering again and again to himself, "Bitch. You bitch."

Bitch . . .

Now, in his office, Hunt finished his drink, memories bitter in his mind.

Lymon Tegler came over from Hardin County whenever Arthur Hunt needed him. Ostensibly a ranch hand, Tegler was in fact a gunman of modest but ferocious skills. If he could not shoot you fairly, he shot you unfairly, and if this bothered him, he never let on.

It was Tegler who'd crouched in the alley that morning when Sheriff John T. Larson had been passing by, and Tegler who'd been trying to shoot at Larson without hitting him. Then the stranger Cage pushed Tegler and the bullet went into Larson's shoulder.

Now Tegler and his men played poker in the smaller of the two bunkhouses on Arthur Hunt's ranch. Hunt's regular men did not want to be anywhere near Tegler. His men were ornery, quick-tempered, and always ready to smash up a cowhand they'd taken some unfathomable dislike to.

Hunt came in the front door of the bunkhouse and watched them playing cards. Tegler and his men had already begun drinking for the evening and this infuriated Hunt. He walked over to the table and snatched up the sour mash bottle they'd been drinking from.

"I told you," Hunt said to Tegler, "no drinking till this is over."

Tegler was a squat man, balding though he was not yet thirty, with an impressive-looking scar angled across his chin. He had flat hard blue eyes and a smile that almost never conveyed pleasure. He said, "Yessir, bossman."

Tegler looked at his three men. They glanced up at Hunt and tittered like schoolchildren. "Yessir, bossman," one of them said in the same mocking tone Tegler had used.

Irritated, Hunt hurled the bottle into the corner. It smashed into three jagged pieces. The aroma of whiskey filled the bunkhouse.

"You remember what you're supposed to do?"

Tegler looked down at his cards. "I remember."

"You've got to make it look good."

Now Tegler looked up. "I ever let you down before, bossman?" He fanned his cards and studied them again. "Never thought a man would hire me to shoot his own son."

"That part of it is none of your business. You just do what I tell you. Jeremy'll have a gun and he'll escape. We'll be in town and see him and then you'll pretend you thought he was drawing down on you and you'll kill him by accident."

"Then I get the second half of the gold." It wasn't a question. "The boys and me want to head for Mexico soon as possible. Hear tell they've got some new twelve-year-old girls all shined up and waitin' for us."

Hunt watched Tegler with a biding disgust. This would be the last time he'd work with the man. The more Tegler drank — and it was more every time they worked together now — the more belligerent and less reliable he became.

"Saddle up," Hunt said.

Tegler glanced again at his men and smirked. "Yessir, bossman; yessir."

Then he gave Hunt a mocking little salute.

Chapter Sixteen

"Did you ever see her hanging out with your father?"

When Cage asked this question, Jeremy Hunt's head snapped up. "What kind of question is that?"

"A question I need to ask."

"Why would my father spend time with a — a girl like Sally Dane. What're you driving at anyway?"

Now that his deputy was back, Cage had taken the opportunity to question Jeremy in the cell. So far, Hunt had been anything but cooperative.

"Lisa seems to think your father may have had something to do with Sally Dane's death."

Instead of shouting, Jeremy just shook his head miserably. He looked up at the bars, beyond which the velvet night sky was beginning to glitter with stars. "She told me that, too," he said in a whisper. "How could she ever think of such a thing?"

"She tells me you don't get along very well with your father."

Jeremy shrugged. "There's a difference between not getting along and — and doing what she's suggesting."

Cage decided to push the kid as far as he'd go. "Are you satisfied your mother's death was really an accident?"

"Of course. Why?"

But Cage could see the doubt play on the kid's face. He stayed silent a long moment and then said, "If you get hanged, Jeremy, your father gets the whole ranch to himself. Have you ever thought of that?"

"He wouldn't have killed my mother."

"The way I'm told it, their marriage hadn't been very good for a long time."

"You're talking about Belle."

"Yes, I suppose I am."

"Well, that happens in marriages, Cage. And in a lot more of them than you'd think."

"If he didn't love your mother, maybe he didn't love you."

"My father's had a hard life. Maybe you don't know about that. His mother died when he was just two and he was raised by a father who beat him every chance he got. If you watch the way my father walks, you'll notice that his left leg kicks out every once in a while. That's because the old man broke my father's hip when he was beating him one day. Do you have any idea how much force it takes to beat a person hard enough to break a hip?"

Cage sat up straight on the edge of the bunk across from young Hunt. "If you didn't kill that girl, and your father didn't kill that girl, then who did?"

"I don't know."

"Even if you don't, you may have to hang for it anyway."

The miserable look came back to the kid's face and his eyes once more went to the sky and the full silver moon framed perfectly in the window of his cell.

"He didn't kill her," Jeremy said, keeping his gaze on the sky.

"You don't really believe that, do you? You're starting to have doubts but you can't quite let yourself believe them, isn't that it?"

Jeremy swung his head around and faced Cage. "Do I ever get any dinner in this place, Cage?"

"Juanita's supposed to be here in a few minutes." Cage, shaking his head, stood up. Pulling the keys out of his pocket, he slipped his hand through the bars and opened the door. He stepped out of the cell and locked it up again.

"Would you rather hang than admit the

possibility that your father murdered that girl and fixed it up so you'd be accused of it?"

Anger and pride played on the kid's face now. He said, "All I want from you is some dinner, Cage. That's all."

Cage went back to the front office, where his deputy sat.

Chapter Seventeen

As a small girl, Lisa had been told to stay away from the neighborhood that bordered the tracks. Parents were filled with dark tales of children who'd been gobbled up by the nightfall denizens of this place.

But as she grew older, Lisa saw that the only spooks that inhabited the neighborhood were the spooks of poverty and filth and despair. The people here were Chinese and Mexican and Indian, and while she pitied them and their lot, she feared them, too. Oh, not in the way a person feared goblins but rather in the way a person feared desperate people who envied and resented your own station in life.

Only rarely did she ever come down here and certainly not after nightfall.

But tonight — her fears for Jeremy almost overwhelming her — she walked these streets without feeling any intimidation whatsoever.

Her mind was racing too fast to be intimidated.

Most of the "houses" were, in fact,

shacks. Starving dogs ran between these shacks and yipped at her. Babies bawled. Men sat out in front of their shacks drinking warm beer from buckets. Even though it was dark, a few children ran around in noisy circles, playing games.

She had no address. She had been told by a bartender that Sally Dane's sister lived in the last house on the right side of the street, the house closest to the spur in the tracks.

A few men whistled at her as she made her way quickly through the darkness, nearly tripping over cans and other refuse that had been left to fill up the street.

Ahead now, she saw a light burning inside a little shack set apart from the others. The stench of rotting garbage seemed to grow stronger the closer she got. She held her breath, the stench momentarily unbearable.

"You wan' some fun tonight, seester," a male voice called to her from the shadows. And then chuckled.

She hurried on her way to the last house and, when she reached the front of it, went immediately up to the door, around the edges of which she could see the soft glow of lamplight.

She knocked, turning her neck to see if anybody had followed her up here. For the first time, she sensed that this neighbor-hood represented great danger to a woman like herself.

Nobody answered the knock.

Inside, she heard someone nudge against furniture. Then there was silence. Obviously someone was hiding, unwilling to answer the knock.

"Hello," Lisa said. "Please answer the door."

Nothing.

Lisa thought — or imagined anyway — that she could hear the faint sounds of breathing.

She had an image of someone hiding in a corner of the small shack, waiting for Lisa to give up finally and leave.

But with Jeremy in trouble, there was no way Lisa was going to do that.

She knocked again.

Somewhere behind her, in the darkness, male voices laughed and one called out to her, "I don' theenk she wan' to see you, white lady."

More laughter.

"Please, Gretta, answer the door," Lisa said.

Again nothing.

This time Lisa tried the doorknob.

Unlocked.

She pushed the slab of plywood inward, hearing it creak on unoiled joints.

The shack was about what she would have expected. Two or three pieces of rudimentary furniture, including a daybed; a table busy with flies playing around rotted fruit and meat; and a large painting of a sad and solemn Jesus that seemed to dominate the entire western wall.

No sign of anyone.

Lisa went inside, closing the creaking door behind her.

The stench was bad but not overwhelming. She decided to look around the one-room shack. She checked behind the small couch and then behind the plump, ragged armchair.

"Gretta," she called several times.

Finally she stood in the center of the room, staring down at the daybed.

There was only one place the girl could be.

A comforter lay across the bed, touching the floor. The comforter would hide anybody who had crawled under the bed.

Lisa went over and stood above the bed. "I know where you are, Gretta. Please come out."

The response was so quick it startled her. "Go away." The voice was muffled by the comforter.

"You know something about your sister's murder, don't you? Something that's making you afraid."

Nothing.

"I'll see to it that nobody hurts you," Lisa said. "I promise."

"I can't talk to you. Go away. They'll find out you were here and then they'll come after me."

"You don't have to be afraid, Gretta. I can see that you're protected."

Gretta said nothing.

Suddenly the daybed was jostled. A slender feminine hand appeared first. Then the arm.

In another half-minute, a small, pretty, but very shabby girl of perhaps seventeen had crawled out from under the bed. She had stringy brown hair, a dirty face, and a dress made from worn cotton. She wore no shoes. Lisa could smell how badly the girl needed to bathe.

"I can't tell you anything," Gretta Dane said. "You know what they did to my sister."

"Don't you want to see the person who killed your sister be hanged for it?"

The girl shook her head. "What difference does it make? She's dead, isn't she? Even if the right person did hang for it, it wouldn't bring her back."

She walked over to the table and picked up a half-filled bottle of wine, brushing flies away from the fruit and meat as she did so. She tilted the bottle toward Lisa, who shook her head no.

"It was Arthur Hunt, wasn't it?"

Gretta Dane paused in the middle of her drinking and said, "It's no use, Miss Tate. I'm not going to talk to you." She swigged down some more wine.

"Do you want me to tell you how much I love Jeremy?"

The girl stared at her a long moment. "I've loved a lot of people in my life, too, Miss Tate. That didn't stop them from having bad things happen to them. Why should you be different from me?" For the first time, her tone was bitter. Her eyes looked with distaste at Lisa's pretty frock and Lisa's pretty face. Lisa wanted to explain to her that Gretta could look just as good, if only she'd begin taking care of herself.

But now wasn't the time.

"Arthur Hunt lured your sister up into that hotel room, didn't he?"

Gretta Dane just stared at her.

"Or was it Sam Jenkins, Gretta? I found an envelope in his pocket with your sister's name and the amount of two hundred dollars written on it. Was that what they paid her?"

Gretta went back to swigging wine.

"What did they tell her? That Jeremy needed to be with a woman that night? Did they convince her that this was just a simple little job and that she'd be given the whole two hundred dollars once Jeremy was satisfied?"

Gretta put the bottle down. "Get out, you bitch. I don't like you in my house with your expensive clothes and your arrogant looks."

For the first time, Lisa realized the girl was drunk.

"That is what happened, isn't it? They got her in the room and then they killed her — really butchered her, Gretta, remember that — and then they brought in Jeremy. He was already drunk but they poured more alcohol down him so he'd forget everything . . . and then they let the deputy know that something was going on in the room. So he walked in and found Jeremy there with your sister in the closet."

Gretta slapped her.

The blow was quick and clean, and for a long moment, Lisa's head reeled and she was afraid she was going to pass out.

"I told you, bitch, to get out of here,"

Gretta said. "Or I'll really slap you around."

You would not think that such a frail body could be capable of so much rage or physical violence. But you would be wrong.

"Get out," she said again before Lisa's head had had a chance to clear.

This time, she pushed Lisa hard into the doorway, slamming her head against the doorframe.

"Bitch," Gretta said, and shoved Lisa outside.

A moment later she slammed the door.

Somewhere in the spinning night — her stomach threatening to boil up in her — Lisa heard the male voices taunting her in the darkness.

"Gretta's hard to make the frien's with," one man said, giggling. " 'Less you got the money."

Another voice: "She call you a bad name, seester?"

Still another: "She call you a beetch? A nice girl like you?"

Then the laughter started in earnest again as Lisa stumbled her way through the darkness.

Chapter Eighteen

Juanita came in with Jeremy's dinner just after six-thirty.

At the time, Cage and Deputy Ron Sorenson were in the front office, their feet up on their respective desks, smoking cigarettes and drinking scalding hot coffee. For the previous fifteen minutes, Cage had been telling Sorenson about why he'd given up being a lawman. As always, the story was simple to recount but complicated to deal with: Entrusted with the life of a young man whom he'd made his deputy, the son of the marshal for whom Cage had once been deputy, Cage and the kid had been prowling down an alley one night when they'd happened on two thieves breaking into the rear of a general store. The thieves had panicked, opened fire, and killed the kid before Cage could get his footing. Knowing how seriously the kid had been wounded there in the moonlight, a kind of madness had come over Cage and he'd walked toward the two men with both his guns drawn, firing into the shadows where he suspected they were hiding. He had not stopped firing until his guns were empty. When he found them, he saw that he'd killed them many times over. His only regret was that he didn't have more bullets to pump into them.

In that town, in that time, things were never the same again for Cage. Oh, people made a show of understanding how things like that happened — how a fine young man could get himself gunned down by two grizzled punks — but always in their voices was just the slightest suspicion that maybe the whole incident might have been prevented somehow if Cage had only been —

If Cage had only been what? That was the question Cage asked himself again and again as he did his best to talk to people, to explain.

If only Cage had been —

Then the nightmares started and Cage knew he'd come to the end of something. Now, not even sleep was an escape, for lying on his bed at night, the moonlight horrors came back to him again and again until he lost the heart and the ability to be town marshal any longer.

Finally, one day he went to the town council and just packed it in. He could see the relief in their eyes. Cage had had real stature in that town before the kid had gotten himself killed, but afterward — Afterward, there was always that vague suspicion about Cage's role in the whole matter. Had he been alert enough? Had he maybe had a drink or two that night? (He hadn't.) Had he —

The questions were endless but now Cage had made them irrelevant by resigning.

Then he'd wired his brother outside Yuma that he was coming to take up his brother's long-standing offer of helping Cage become a rancher.

He took his carpetbag and his two guns, and then he was gone, his five-pointed star lying in the bottom of a drawer back in the sheriff's office, awaiting a new man.

"Evening, Ron," Juanita said as she sidled through the front door, carrying a tray covered with several checkered napkins so the food would stay warm.

"Evening, Juanita. You met Mr. Cage yet?"

"Haven't had the pleasure," Juanita said. "Evenin' to you, too, Mr. Cage."

Cage stood up and doffed his hat. "Take it that's for the prisoner?"

Juanita smiled out of a worn face. "Some

people say my cookin's a worse punishment than the gallows."

Ron Sorenson laughed. "It's bad, Juanita, but it ain't that bad."

Cage stepped over to her and put his hands on either side of the tray. "Here, Juanita, why don't you let me take that into him for you?"

She tightened her grip on the tray, her eyes flicking to Sorenson. "Oh, I always take it in, don't I, Ron?"

"Guess she does, Cage."

Juanita forced a laugh. "Guess even a condemned man deserves to see a pretty face once in a while."

"I'd be happy to take it in for you," Cage said.

"Appreciate the offer, Mr. Cage. But I'll be fine."

Cage dropped his hands from the tray and went over to the cell block door, easing it back so Juanita could pass through.

"Thank you very much, Mr. Cage," Juanita said, and disappeared inside the cell block.

Cage went over to the gun rack, checking the carbines for the fourth time already this evening. He knew that by midnight, he'd have call to use some of these guns and he wanted to make sure they were ready. As his hands worked among the carbines, he kept thinking about Juanita's frozen smile and the way her voice had gotten very tight when he'd put his hands on the tray.

Cage said, "You known Juanita long?"

"Sure. Lot of years. She grew up around here and so did I. Why?"

"You trust her?"

The deputy shrugged. "Never thought about it much, I guess."

"So you do trust her?"

"I reckon."

"She act kind of funny tonight, you think?"

"Funny how?"

"Maybe a little scared. You see her when I put my hands on that tray?"

"Guess I didn't notice."

"She tensed up pretty good there. Looked scared."

The deputy shook his head, smiled. "You've sure got some imagination."

"Maybe so."

He went back to checking the carbines.

"Evening, Jeremy."

Jeremy lay on his back on the narrow

bunk and just looked at her. His face was silver from the moonlight.

"Got a real nice dinner for you here, Jeremy."

Talk of food made him sit up.

"Got to hand it through the slot there," Juanita said. "You ready?"

He nodded and rose to stand by the cell door. He rubbed his face as if he'd just awakened.

Juanita pushed the tray through.

He took it over to his bunk and set it down.

She leaned up to the bars and whispered, "Your pa sent you a gift."

"A gift?"

"Sssh. Not so loud."

"What kind of gift?"

"Lift up the napkin and look."

The first napkin Jeremy lifted revealed two legs of fried chicken. The next napkin revealed boiled potatoes and corn. The third napkin revealed a Navy Colt.

Jeremy looked up at her. He was excited. "You tell him thanks."

She leaned into the bars again, her eyes glancing anxiously at the cell door behind her. "He'll meet you out behind the livery in half an hour. He's goin' to help you escape."

Jeremy came up from the bunk. You could see how the excitement was pumping new energy through his slender body. "They're not going to get their chance to hang me. I knew he'd come through for me."

"Why wouldn't he come through for you, Jeremy? He's your pa." She looked back at the door. "I'd better be gettin' out of here."

He took her wrist with more force than he'd intended. "Thank you, Juanita. You're a true friend."

"You just hightail it out of here, soon as you get the chance."

Jeremy grinned. "You don't have to worry about that, Juanita. You don't have to worry about that at all."

She nodded and walked back down the short stretch of corridor till she reached the cell block door. She knocked.

Cage got the door. "He happy about his meal?"

"Like a kid," Juanita said, coming through into the front office. "Just like a kid."

Cage watched her carefully. "Everything all right?"

She switched her gaze to him anxiously.

"Sure, Mr. Cage. Everything's fine. Why?"

"You just seem a little nervous is all."

The forced laugh again. "Jail bars always make me nervous." She spoke across to Ron: "How's your wife?"

"Fine," the deputy said, though by now you could see that he also sensed something wrong with her.

"Well," she said, and eased on over to the front door. "Guess I'll be seein' you gents."

The two men stared at each other and back at her.

She put a hand on the knob.

Cage, without a word, grabbed her wrist. "You care to tell me what's going on?"

She made a face. "You're hurting me."

"I mean to hurt you."

"Nothing's going on. Nothing."

"You brought him something, didn't you?"

"No."

Cage turned her wrist some more. "The truth."

"No — yes. Please don't hurt me anymore."

"What did you bring him?"

"A gun."

"Who told you to?"

"It was my idea."

He twisted her arm hard again. "Who told you to?"

"Owww. Please, Mr. Cage. Please."

"You heard me."

"It was my own idea. Honest." She glanced over at the deputy for help. "Can't you stop him?"

Ron grinned. "He's the sheriff, Juanita, not me."

"Come on now, Juanita," Cage said. "Whose idea was it?"

"You know who."

"Arthur Hunt's?"

"I didn't tell you anything. Remember that. I didn't tell you anything." Then she told him how Sam had come over. "Now will you quit hurting me?"

He let go of her arm.

To the deputy, he said, "Cover me."

"If he's got a gun, you don't want to go in there," the deputy said reasonably enough.

"You got any better ideas?"

Ron kind of half smiled. "Not if you put it that way."

Cage looked at Juanita and nodded to the front door. "Get out of here. Go straight back to the restaurant and don't say a word to anybody. You understand?"

She was still rubbing her wrist from

where he'd squeezed it. She nodded that she understood.

"Go," Cage said.

She went out the door, closing it quietly. The deputy had taken two carbines from the gun rack. He tossed one to Cage and kept the other for himself.

"You're covered," the deputy said.

Cage pulled the squeaking door back. "Jeremy," he said loudly. His voice echoed off the stone walls of the cell block.

"What do you want?"

"We found out what Juanita brought you."

"Juanita didn't bring me anything."

"She brought you a gun, Jeremy."

"She didn't bring me anything."

"She brought you a gun and that wasn't a very smart thing to do on her part."

Jeremy said nothing.

"You know who had her bring the gun?"

Nothing.

Cage kept himself pressed flat against the right side of the door. He flung his words into the darkness the way he might later have to fling bullets.

"Your father told her to bring the gun, Jeremy."

"If that's true," Jeremy shouted, "I guess that proves you were all wrong about my father wanting me to be hanged, doesn't it?"

"What if it's a trap?"

Long silence. "What?"

"What if it's a trap?"

"What if your father wants you to escape so one of his men can kill you?"

"Why would he do that?"

"Because that would be the easiest way to get rid of you. There wouldn't even have to be a trial. Everybody would just assume that you'd been shot by accident and that you died guilty of killing Sally Dane."

"My father wouldn't do anything like that."

Cage hesitated, knowing how deeply his next words would cut. As they'd cut the first time he'd asked Jeremy this question. "You ever ask yourself how your mother really died, Jeremy?"

"You sonofabitch," Jeremy said. "You said that before. What the hell are you trying to say?"

"You know what I'm trying to say, Jeremy. You know what I'm trying to say because you've had the same thoughts yourself, haven't you?"

"Why don't you come in here and try to take this gun from me, Cage?"

"Don't be crazy, Jeremy. I've got a carbine here."

"Yeah, but it's dark and you can't see what you're doing."

Cage, who'd been readying himself for his move for several minutes, whirled into the open doorway, dropped to one knee, and got two shots off before Jeremy even had a chance to fire.

Cage had a pretty good sense of where Jeremy was so he didn't think he'd inflict a mortal wound. But as Jeremy's cry indicated, Cage had hit something.

In the moonlit shadows of the cell block, a handgun clattered to the floor.

Cage rushed into the cell block, his carbine at the ready. The deputy was right behind him.

"Jeremy?" Cage said.

"You sonofabitch," Jeremy said from the floor of his cell.

"Where'd I get you?"

"Leg," Jeremy said between gritted teeth. "Right leg."

Cage got the cell door open. "You're a lot luckier than you think, kid. A lot luckier."

The deputy ran to get the doc.

Chapter Nineteen

In the old days, back when the ranch was first growing, Arthur Hunt had come to the Golden Coin because it was the saloon where his men liked to raise hell on Saturday nights. The Coin, as it came to be known, had women, music, and the sort of bartenders who let men play rough but not get hurt too seriously. The owner — a man named Drake, who'd died a few years back — had been smart enough to put all his money in the bank and none into fixing the place up. For a long time, Hunt had thought this was a sensible idea — what was the point in fixing up a place like the Coin?

But tonight as he and Lymon Tegler and the other eight men had come into the Coin, Hunt had been struck by what a dump the place was — wooden floors slick and brown with tobacco juice, walls with a myriad of filthy words scrawled on them, mirrors with cracks held together with tape. The Coin was a sink hole and Arthur Hunt could no longer tolerate it.

They had been in there twenty minutes

— two beers down apiece — when word came about the shooting at the jail.

Hunt grabbed the sleeve of the crippled man bringing the news. "What happened?"

"Shooting at the jail, Mr. Hunt," the man said, intimidated by the mere presence of someone like Arthur Hunt.

"Who got shot?" For a wild moment, Hunt allowed himself to think that his work had perhaps been done for him — Jeremy, in a hurry to escape, had been shot dead by the deputy or the acting sheriff Cage.

The crippled man, whose right foot had been crushed by a wagon when he was very young, gulped and said, "Your son."

"Shot bad?"

The man gulped again. "In the leg is all."

Hunt didn't dare show his disappointment. He let the man's sleeve go and he said, "Thanks for telling me."

The man, trembling, nodded and went over to the bar.

Tegler said, "Sounds like we're gonna have to make some new plans, Art. Your son ain't gonna make it behind the livery stable now."

One of Tegler's men said, "We're gonna have to take the jail and git him ourselves."

He spoke with real enthusiasm. This was the kind of thing Tegler's men enjoyed. The only talent these crude, simple men possessed was in shooting up places and scaring people. They were just smart enough to know that it was the only thing on this earth that made them valuable.

Hunt fixed the man with an angry gaze. "I'm afraid you're right."

The man glanced at his companions and grinned.

"But first," Hunt said, "I'll try and reason with this Cage fellow."

The grin vanished from the man's face.

"I don't think he'll want to get shot his first day on the job," Hunt said.

Tegler shrugged. "Never can tell. Lawmen are a funny breed."

Hunt looked at Tegler. Hunt wanted to laugh. If lawmen were a "funny breed," what did that make Tegler and his men? Who could make sense of a life that consisted of shooting people and razing small towns?

"You go with me," Hunt said to Tegler. "Bring a carbine."

"What about us?" one of the other men said, sounding like a disappointed child.

"You stay here," Hunt said. "No need for you right now."

The man glowered at Hunt.

"Come on," Hunt said.

As soon as Hunt had reached town, word went out that he was here with rough men to take his son back. Houses that had been dark suddenly lit up with kerosene lamps and men who had been snuggling in bed with their wives suddenly found themselves trembling and anxious. There was no doubt where the appearance of Arthur Hunt and his men could leave them. In the old days, townspeople had often had to stand up against the ravages of outlaws and men bent on corrupt power. You heard tale after tale of how butchers had joined with blacksmiths, who had in turn joined with clerics to pick up hunting rifles to stand off invaders. Trouble was, those were the old days. Willow Creek was civilized now and men were no longer inclined to the rough justice of the past. That was why towns got together and hired lawmen. That was why towns got together and had militia. Because the men of the town did not want to be wakened and told they had to roll out into the chill crisp autumn night, rubbing sleep from their eyes, and take on the grizzled likes of Arthur Hunt's hired guns.

So after several men went door-to-door

informing men of Hunt's appearance, there were hurried and hushed conversations in darkened bedrooms as wives talked husbands out of joining in any sort of mob to stand against Hunt. The wives didn't have to talk too long or too hard.

Let that new lawman take care of it, honey, the wives said.

Well, said the husbands. If you insist.

You've got to think of the children; how would they be without a pa, the wives said.

You're right, the husbands said. You're absolutely right.

So the lamps were blown back out and the couples went back to their beds. They were charitable enough to say a few prayers for the man named Cage and his deputy.

God knew, those two poor men were going to need all the prayers they could get.

Chapter Twenty

Cage poured himself a cup of coffee and walked back to the desk where the doc was sitting. "He going to be all right?" Cage asked.

"Not much of a wound as wounds go," the doc said. "He'll be fine." The doc sipped his own coffee. "Can't say his father's going to be thrilled by the news, though. You heard he was in town?"

Cage nodded. "The deputy went to see if he could round some men up."

The doc made a face. "I wouldn't bet on recruiting anybody in this town. One reason John T. got so powerful is that people here are willing to let lawmen do pretty much what they want — as long as none of the townspeople get involved in the violence."

Cage said, "I heard Hunt's got eight toughs over to the Golden Coin."

"They'd be Lymon Tegler's men." The doc sipped some coffee. "Not the kind of men you'd enjoy facing down, if you don't mind my saying so."

Cage went over to the barred window and looked out on the nighttime street. It was nearing midnight now and the street was empty. From far away in the shadows, you could hear the honky-tonk sounds of saloons and taverns. "Don't reckon I'll be facing anybody down." He turned around and faced the doc. "Figure they'll make a rush for the jail so they can spring the kid back there."

"Guess that makes sense."

The doc stood up and set his coffee down. He stuffed a spool of clean white medical wrapping in his small black bag, fixed his black bowler on his bald head, and went over to the door. "Got two patients come down with anthrax about twenty miles outside of town."

"Have to go see them tonight?"

"Afraid I do, yes." The doc looked at the rifle rack. "Hope you get some more help, Mr. Cage. To be honest, you're going to need it. Art Hunt ain't going to take kindly to you shooting his boy, no matter how slight the wound was."

No, Cage thought. He'll probably be mad because I didn't kill his boy. That way he'd get the ranch free and clear.

"We'll see how it goes," Cage said, and nodded good-bye to the doc.

153

"He's going to try and take you, Jeremy. He's in town and he's got eight toughs with him."

Jeremy sat up on the bunk. He couldn't keep the glee from his eyes.

Cage, standing outside the cell door with a lantern in his hand, said, "If I were you, Jeremy, I wouldn't go with him, even if he gets in here and sets you free."

Jeremy rubbed his face. "You're still working on your tired old theory about my father wanting to kill me? We've had our differences, Pa and I, but you can see that he cares about me. Otherwise why would he bring eight toughs to town?"

"Lisa knows the truth."

"Lisa's just skittish and her imagination works overtime."

Cage sighed. "Unless Ron Sorenson and I get some help, we won't be able to hold them off."

"My father isn't the type to shoot somebody in cold blood."

What about your mother? Cage wanted to say but he stopped himself. "I'd really think hard about letting your father take you out of here, kid. I'd think real hard about it."

When he got back to the front office, Cage put the lantern down on the shelf, went over and grabbed himself a carbine and turned around just in time to see his deputy push open the front door and come inside.

"How'd you do?" Cage said.

"Not so good, I'm afraid."

"Nobody willing to help?"

"They've all got one excuse or another. Not feeling well or wives won't let them or got too many young'uns at home to risk going up against Art Hunt."

Cage set the carbine down on the desk. "Going to be a long night."

"Yeah," the deputy said. "Real long." He went over to the gun case himself.

The door opened for a second time in as many minutes.

In the doorway was framed a large, theatrical-looking man in a fringe leather jacket and a tall white Stetson. He looked impressive until you studied him briefly and then you saw how pale white his face was.

"Evening, boys. Heard you needed some help and thought I'd offer my services."

Sheriff John T. Larson, as ever larger than life, came ambling into the office,

155

trying to effect a manly swagger.

Unfortunately, when he got even with the first desk, he crumpled up and fell straight down to the floor.

Cage and the deputy both lunged for the older man, dragging him up into a chair. The deputy took a bottle of rye whiskey from a desk drawer, held it under Larson's nose like smelling salts, and kept saying the sheriff's name again and again.

"Well, I'll say one thing for the old man," Cage said, once Larson started to revive, "even with a serious wound he's got a lot more guts than most men in this town."

Larson sat up straight in his chair abruptly, seized the bottle of rye from the deputy's hand, and poured what seemed like six ounces straight down his throat.

"Now, boys," he said, "you go get me a carbine."

Both Cage and the deputy started laughing out loud. One thing you had to say for John T. — not even close proximity to death could slow him down.

Inside the closet, Lisa pressed her ear to the door, listening to the first faint footfalls that brought Sam Jenkins nearer to his room.

Sam, Lisa knew, would never expect her

to be hiding in the same closet where he'd discovered her only recently. But that's exactly what she was doing.

There was only one difference. This time she had armed herself with the .44 her father had carried the latter years of his life. In her frail hand, the weapon was heavy and smelled of grease. Despite her awkwardness in handling it, however, Lisa knew she would be able to use it if and when the time came.

The closet smelled of clothes stale with sweat and dirt and of mothballs set in either corner of the small room.

Footsteps. Closer.

Closer.

Lisa readied the .44.

Sam came in and immediately got a kerosene lamp going. The lamp smelled oily on the night air.

Next came the sound of Sam putting his considerable bulk down on the bed. You could hear the mattress groan then Sam groan as he took off his shoes and socks.

Next came his shirt and trousers. He wore no undershirt of any kind. His huge hairy stomach hung jiggling. She saw all this through the keyhole.

What Sam did next surprised her.

Rather than toss himself into bed, he got down on his knees with great slow reverence, bowed his head, made a church steeple of his hands, and proceeded to pray.

Feeling almost like a heathen, she eased open the door and crossed the room to Sam before he had time to turn around.

She jammed the .44 right up against his head.

"Evening, Sam," she said.

His first instinct was to be embarrassed. He wore only huge and wrinkled drawers.

"What the hell're you doing here, Lisa?"

"I came to talk to you."

"About what?"

"You know about what, Sam."

"Lisa, you're gettin' involved in something's that downright dangerous. You know that, don't you?"

"He killed Sally Dane, didn't he?"

"I don't know who you're talking about, Lisa."

"You know darn good and well, Sam. I'm talking about your cousin Arthur Hunt."

"Jeremy killed her."

"You're lying, Sam." She pushed the gun to his forehead.

"Just be careful with that thing." A

158

whining tone had come into his voice. It was almost comical.

"He killed his wife, too, didn't he?"

"Lisa — the gun."

"You think I'd be foolish enough to shoot you accidentally, Sam? Oh no, if I shoot you, I want to have the pleasure of doing it on purpose. You understand me, Sam?"

"Lisa — please. This is an awfully embarrassing position I'm in. All I'm wearing is —"

"I could care less about modesty right now, Sam. Now, tell me everything that happened."

"But Lisa —"

Her strength surprised her. She laid the barrel of the gun across his right cheek, opening up a long, wide gash.

He made a sound that was half a moan and half muffled tears. "Lisa —" he said and you could tell he'd been completely shocked by what she'd just done to him.

"Now stand up, Sam."

"What?"

"Stand up."

"But all I'm wearing is —"

She raised the weapon as if she were going to lay it across his cheek again.

He struggled to his feet. His hairy belly jiggled. He kept shaking his head in disgust and disbelief. He lost all moral standards around whores, but around a proper young woman, he was bashful as an eight-year-old.

"Now, drop your drawers."

"What?" he said, astonished.

"Drop them."

"But Lisa —"

"If you don't choose to drop them, then I want you to tell me about the killings. First Arthur Hunt's wife and then Sally Dane."

"Aw, Lisa, you really wouldn't make me drop them, would you?"

She nudged the gun into his face again. "You're bleeding pretty hard from that cheek, Sam. That should tell you if I'm fooling or not."

He looked at her and then down at his drawers and then he said, "If I tell you the truth, Lisa, he'll kill us both. I swear to God he will."

"I'm willing to take that chance."

Sorrowful Sam, who looked like a beagle that had just lost his best friend, went over and sat down on the bed and daubed at his cheek wound with his fingers.

"I guess it had to come out sometime,"

he said. "Guess now's as good a time as any."

He told her the truth.

All of it.

Chapter Twenty-one

Two shots of whiskey seemed to do well by John T. Larson. Immediately after finishing the second of the drinks, color began returning to his cheeks and his blue eyes shone with clarity.

"I'm fine now," Larson said, sitting up straight in the chair next to his desk. "All I needed was a little help."

Cage smiled at Larson's calling the liquor "help." "So you feel good enough to sit here and face down Hunt and his men?"

"I don't see anybody else around except Sorenson here and you. That makes me a pretty important asset to you, I'd say." From inside a desk drawer, Larson took a fancy, pearl-handled six-shooter, sighting down it then laying it on the desk top. "Hand me a carbine over there, will you, Ron?"

"You really feel up to it, John T.?"

"I walked over here under my own power, didn't I?"

Sorenson glanced at Cage. Cage

shrugged. "You want to go back and lie down on a bunk?"

Larson smiled at such a prospect. "You know how many people would like to see me in one of my own cells?"

"You know what I mean, Larson. Get some rest before the shooting starts."

"I don't want to miss anything," Larson said. Even though color had returned to his face and his voice was almost as deep and resonant as usual, the big man with the flowing white hair displayed signs of age and weakness. His fingers trembled when they touched the six-shooter. His breathing was rapid and shallow. "You know how long I've waited for this?"

Cage shrugged. "Long time, I suppose."

"You know how it's stuck in my craw that that sonofabitch Art Hunt not only married the woman I loved but then killed her on top of it? I've waited a long time for my vengeance and I mean to get it tonight."

"He's got Lymon Tegler and his men with him," Sorenson pointed out.

"Hell, if we can't handle an alcoholic punk like Lymon Tegler, we shouldn't be in the business of law enforcement now, should we?" This sounded very much like the John T. of old. Strong, theatrical, boastful.

Cage grinned. "Hell if they get close enough, John T., maybe you can just talk 'em to death."

Larson didn't seem in the least upset by Cage's ironic remark. "Tell him about the Indian chief, Ron."

Sorenson rolled his eyes and said, "John T. once talked an entire war party out of razing our little burg here. He talked for an hour and a half nonstop and the chief didn't have any idea of what he was saying —"

"But," John T. interrupted, "he was so impressed by my erudition and by the fact that I could talk so long nonstop, that he hied his braves back to the hills and left us alone."

"I'm impressed," Cage said. "Except I don't think Arthur Hunt's going to be."

"Well," Larson said, "just in case he isn't, I've always got this."

With a steady hand, he raised the six-shooter and pointed it dead-center at the front door.

Cage had to admit it — weak as he was, the old man sure looked impressive just now.

"Where we going?"

"Just put your trousers on and you'll find out."

Lisa Tate and Sam Jenkins were still in Sam's hotel room. Lisa still held a gun on him.

In the past fifteen minutes, he had told Lisa enough to see that Arthur Hunt would be the one going to the gallows and not Jeremy.

"Art's out there tonight," Sam said. "If he sees us together, he'll know I talked to you."

"Right now I just want to hurry and get us over to the sheriff's office. You'll be safe there."

"Against Lymon Tegler? Lisa, you don't have any appreciation for what a low-born skunk that man is. Not to mention the men he always has along with him." Sam shook his head. "Lisa, when they make a run for that jail, a lot of lives're going to be lost."

"You haven't met Mr. Cage then. He looks like he can handle himself."

"Maybe he can under normal circumstances. But against Lymon Tegler?" Sam once again shook his head.

"Your pants, Sam. Get into them."

Making a dour face, Sam first pulled on his trousers and then his shirt and then his suitjacket.

Lisa waved the gun at him again. "Now I'm going to take you over to Mr. Cage and I want you to tell him everything you told me. You understand?"

He stared at her. "You sure don't have any pity for me, do you, Lisa?"

Lisa stared right back at him. "Did you have any pity for Jeremy, Sam? Seems to me you were perfectly willing to let him hang for a murder he didn't commit."

There wasn't a lot Sam Jenkins could say to that.

Belle had tried to go to sleep early with the help of a sleeping powder she'd ordered from Sears and three hefty drinks of scotch. For a time, she'd drifted off into a sweaty, troubled sleep filled with nightmares of a beautiful young woman mysteriously becoming a charred, ashen hag with the face of a skeleton and the keening voice of an animal in pain. The hag, dressed in a flowing white wedding gown, walked down the center of Main Street. Men, women, and children ran screaming from her path.

But always Belle woke up, lying there in her chilly sweat and the gloom of the bedroom, thinking about the nightmare and what it meant.

Actually, its meaning was pretty obvious and took no great analysis.

She had come to town as a beautiful

young woman eager for a proper married life once she found the right man. Instead, she'd met Arthur Hunt and, despite her great reluctance, had become his mistress. The years went by and Art made numerous promises but the only thing that changed during this time was the image she saw in her mirror every day. At first, the erosion of her beauty hadn't been so obvious and she was able to delude herself that nobody else noticed the little tracks and wrinkles around her eyes and mouth and the way her lovely breasts had begun to sag slightly and the small fleshy deposit just beneath her otherwise perfect chin.

Middle age.

It came inevitably to everyone.

Belle had been no exception.

Then, no matter what lies she told herself, she was able to see that men indeed perceived her as an aging beauty. Now, men always stared at younger women. Now, men always flirted with others and not Belle.

All she had was Art Hunt.

He'd confided to her his plans, how he would get rid of both his wife and his son. She had been stunned by his coldness. He seemed to have no affection for either of them. All he could talk about was how he'd been so poor when he was young and how he would go to his grave a rich man, the sole owner of the largest ranch in this part of the state.

And she would share it with him.

She had no real idea of who the young woman was nor where Art had met her nor how long things had been going on before Art told her about the girl.

All she knew was that she'd never seen Art like this. She was almost embarrassed for him — potbellied, balding, given to uncouth grunts and groans when he should have been speaking civilized words. "I worship her, Belle," he'd said. "I can't help it."

Art was in love.

No schoolboy had ever looked happier or more foolish.

And Belle was out of his life.

A nightmare hag in a flowing white wedding gown.

Causing people to scream and flee from her.

Now, she sat up in bed and stared at the shadows that played on her walls.

Alone.

She felt so alone.

Art would have it all. The ranch he'd

lusted for all his life. The young woman. Everything.

How many times had she been tempted to march over to John T. Larson's office and tell him the whole story, put Art where he belonged — on the gallows.

But always some crazy hope stopped her — an optimism that was just as foolish as Art's puppy love for the young woman.

Art would change his mind.

Throw over the young woman.

Come back to Belle.

Aging Belle.

But now she knew better.

She could have talked to Cage tonight. Told him everything.

She had nothing left. She might as well have the satisfaction of vengeance.

Almost without realizing what she was doing, she fled from her bed as if it were on fire, went over to her closet, and quickly took down a regal street dress.

She was ready to go in less than two minutes, running a brush through her hair and chewing some gum to lessen her bad breath.

Quickly, she wrote a letter on a white, embossed piece of stationery and then sealed the letter in an envelope, tucking it into her purse.

Then she was on the boardwalk and heading straight for the sheriff's office.

She was going to do something she should have done long ago.

Chapter Twenty-two

"I'll be damned," Sorenson said, squinting out the barred window on the street side of the sheriff's office.

"What?" John T. Larson said.

"You won't believe who's walking up here."

"Who?" Cage said.

"Arthur Hunt himself."

"What?" Larson said.

"Yup," Sorenson said.

"He got Lymon Tegler with him?" Larson asked.

"Nope."

"He's alone?"

"Yep."

Cage went to the window and stared out. From all the talk about what a legendary figure Arthur Hunt was in these parts, Cage was almost disappointed in what he saw. The man coming down the dusty street and into the pool of light surrounding the sheriff's office was chunky, middle-aged, and balding. He looked as if he'd be tough enough in some kind of wrestling contest but he sure didn't appear formidable or remarkable in any other way.

"Wonder what the hell he's doin' here," Sorenson said.

"Wants to talk, obviously," Larson said.

"Maybe it's a trap," Sorenson said. "Maybe we open the door and Lymon Tegler and his men start firing from the shadows over there."

"Maybe so," Larson said.

"Only one way to find out," Cage said, hefting his carbine and going to the door. He nodded to the other two. "Now you two step aside."

"I'm sheriff here," Larson said in a theatrical, and wounded, way.

Cage smiled. "Seems I remember you appointing me acting sheriff."

"Well —" Larson said.

"Just let me handle it," Cage said.

He opened the door and stepped outside onto the boardwalk.

When Arthur Hunt saw him, he slowed down and said, "You Cage?"

"That'd be me."

"Wonder if we could talk."

"You armed?"

"Do I look armed?"

"That isn't what I asked you."

Hunt, obviously not used to being addressed in this fashion, said, "No, Mr. Cage, I'm not armed."

"Good, then you can come inside."

Hunt came up closer to the light. "Maybe they haven't told you who I am exactly, Mr. Cage."

Cage grinned. "Oh yes, Mr. Hunt, they've told me who you are — exactly."

He let the implication of his words float on the edgy silence.

Hunt preceded him inside.

Lymon Tegler waited for Hunt half a block away. Tegler and his men lounged against darkened buildings on either side of an alley. The livery was not far away and in the moonlit darkness you could smell road apples from the equine traffic of the day and the last smoking bits of the blacksmith's work.

Tegler was the first to see Belle coming toward the downtown area.

At first he didn't know who she was, of course, just a woman whose perfume from even a few hundred feet away was a welcome relief from the road apples.

In her long white dress she was like an apparition in the gloom.

When she came closer, he recognized her

immediately. Art Hunt's castoff and former mistress.

Tegler grinned.

During the war, he had made rape a specialty. Never was a farm burned or a hamlet razed without Tegler finding a woman to sate his needs. "Woman" was used loosely by Tegler. He had taken "women" as young as eleven and as old as eighty. Indeed, he found the extreme in ages to be almost as erotic as the rape itself. A few of them he'd killed, slashing their throats when he was through with them.

Now, he said, "Well, if it ain't Miss High-and-Mighty."

Belle had been moving along the boardwalk with her head down. Hurrying somewhere obviously.

Now she glanced up and in the darkness you could see real fear in her eyes.

She had always hated Tegler. Every time Art Hunt had brought the man around, Belle had found a way to spurn and demean him. He was a man who hated women and Belle had always sensed this.

But now, without Art's protection —

"Looks like we're gonna have ourselves some fun, boys," Tegler said, pushing away from the building he'd been leaning against.

He reached out and grabbed Belle by the shoulder, slamming her up against the wall.

"Don't have Art around to protect you any more, do you?" Tegler said. "Got hisself a new woman." He looked around at his men and laughed. "Young one with firm flesh."

He reached out and grabbed her breast, twisting it. "Not sagging the way you are these days, Belle."

"Let me go, Tegler," Belle said, obviously summoning her rage. She could not, however, keep the fear from her eyes or her words.

"Sure, I'll let you go," Tegler said. "Soon as I get done with you, right, boys?"

His hand snapped out with surprising speed and ripped her dress all the way down the front.

She tried to scream, but he slapped her, slamming her head against the wall.

When she started to sink, already unconscious, something fluttered from her hand to the boardwalk.

A letter.

Lymon Tegler, disregarding Belle for the moment, bent down and picked it up.

He walked down the boardwalk to a lamppost. In the fuzzy golden illumination, he read as much of the letter as he could. He had only gotten through the second grade.

But he could read enough of her words to know what she'd done.

Written a letter to Cage detailing everything she knew about Arthur Hunt.

How he'd killed his wife.

How he'd framed his son.

Lymon Tegler smiled.

He could hear Belle, back up the street, coming back to consciousness, the men muffling her screams.

At first he'd been afraid that Art Hunt would not take kindly to Tegler's plans for Belle.

But after Tegler showed him this letter, Hunt would excuse anything Tegler had elected to do with Belle.

He walked back up the street, the sound of his boots heavy on the boardwalk.

Two of his men held Belle by either wrist in the mouth of the alley. She was struggling hard and starting to cry.

"Let's have ourselves a little fun," Tegler said, sticking the envelope in his shirt. "Leastways, that's what I plan to do."

Chapter Twenty-three

"We can make this real easy," Arthur Hunt said, "for all of us."

Cage, Hunt, John T. Larson, and Sorenson sat in the front office. Cage offered Hunt a cup of coffee but Hunt shook his head.

"I've got just as much of an interest in the welfare of this town as you do, John T.," Hunt went on. "Just because you and I don't get on is no reason for us to tear this town apart."

"What are you after?" Cage said.

Hunt nodded to the cell block door. "You've got my son back there. People in this territory hate me but they can't get to me — so they're going to take it out on my son. I don't believe he killed that girl."

No, he didn't, Cage thought. Because you did.

"You want us to let your son go?"

"I want you to turn him over to me. I'll take him to Lindemere County and turn him over to Judge Hoskins there."

"Your old crony Frank Hoskins?" John T.

177

Larson said, grimacing from where his wound gave him pain. "He'll sure get a fair trial in Lindemere. Hoskins will set him free in twenty-four hours."

"Is he going to get a fair trial in this county, John T.?"

Larson shrugged and stared down at his coffee. "I still want to take him to Cedar County."

"What happens if we don't release him to you?" Cage said.

"I guess you know the answer to that one," Hunt said. He looked first at Sorenson and then at Larson and then back at Cage. "I'm told you didn't have very much luck recruiting men tonight. Which means that you're outnumbered about two-to-one. And you know what Tegler's men are like. You know what they'll do to this town." He shifted his eyes to the cell block door again. "I just want justice for my boy."

Cage looked over to Larson then back to Hunt. "I'm afraid we can't make a deal here tonight, Hunt."

Hunt said, "You ever think you could get killed here tonight?"

"I've considered the fact that it could happen, yes."

"And for a town that's not even yours?"

"I guess I'll have to take that chance."

Hunt said, "John T., you going to talk some sense into this young man's head?"

"Afraid I can't, Art." He smiled. "Guess you and I have had this coming for a lot of years."

"Why take the town down with us? A lot of innocent people could get hurt."

Larson smiled again. "Since when did you ever worry about innocent people, Art?" The smile vanished abruptly. "You didn't worry about your wife bein' innocent when you killed her."

"Doesn't seem like you were ever able to prove that, John T. So I guess it isn't worth talking about." He looked to Cage again. "You ready for trouble, Mr. Cage?"

"Ready as I'll ever be."

"Trouble's what you're going to get."

Cage could see the bully in the man now. "We'll do our best to survive. Suppose you will, too."

"You're not going to change your mind then, Mr. Cage?"

"Afraid not."

Hunt glanced around the office. His eyes fell on Sorenson. "How do you think your wife's going to feel if she loses you, too, Ron? Wasn't losing your son enough?"

Sorenson flushed with anger. "I don't

see where my wife's any concern of yours, Hunt."

Hunt moved back to the front door. "We're going to take him out of here tonight whether you try to stop us or not. No judge in the territory would hold with the kind of kangaroo court you've got in mind for Jeremy."

"You've had your say," Cage said.

"It's a shame to do this to a town as fine as Willow Creek," Hunt said.

Larson laughed. "Well, now, a civics lesson from Arthur Hunt himself. Now isn't that somethin' to think about, boys?"

Now Hunt flushed. "You talk a good game, John T. But I'm afraid you're too old and too weak to do anything more than talk."

With that, he opened the door and went out into the night, leaving the three men to their silence.

"Going to be a long night," Sorenson said, and you could hear the fear in his voice.

John T. Larson said, "Hunt had a point. Irma wouldn't be able to take it if she lost both the boy and you. You're all she's got left, Ron. Maybe you —"

Cage said, "I feel the same way, Ron. You could head on home now and —"

"I'm staying," Sorenson said. "If only to prove to Arthur Hunt that I ain't scared of him. I wouldn't want to give him that satisfaction."

John T. Larson smiled, obviously impressed and pleased with Sorenson's decision. "Like the man said, it's going to be a long night."

Larson couldn't quite keep the note of relish out of his voice.

A couple of times Sam Jenkins tried to whirl around and knock the gun from Lisa Tate's hand but she was always too quick for him.

She took several narrow alleys to the sheriff's office so that none of Hunt's men could see her and stop her.

When she reached the office, she jammed the gun deeper into Sam's back and marched him right up to the door.

Cage, seeing her coming, got the door open and held it so Sam and Lisa could come inside.

"Sam's decided to tell the truth for once in his life," Lisa said, sounding like a schoolmarm chastising a small boy. "Right, Sam?"

Sam Jenkins was clearly embarrassed. Being held captive by a slender young woman

181

was not a position any self-respecting man liked to find himself in.

"Right, Sam?"

She nudged him with the gun again.

"Right," Sam said, averting the amused stares of the other men.

"So tell them what you told me."

"I changed my mind."

"What?"

"I said, Lisa, that I changed my mind. That ain't so hard to understand, is it?"

What she did next startled everybody, probably including herself.

She slammed the barrel of the gun so hard across the back of Sam's head that he was driven to his knees.

Groaning, making faint crying sounds in his throat, Sam looked up at her and said, "You're gettin' mean, Lisa. Awful mean."

"You tell them now, Sam Jenkins, or I'll do it again."

This time Sam met the stares of the other men. He pleaded for mercy.

They weren't about to provide him with any.

"Tell them, Sam," Lisa Tate said again, and raised the gun as if to strike him once more.

Sam decided now would be a good time to start talking.

"You better look at her, Tegler."

"What?"

"That woman. Belle."

"What about her?"

"You better look at her."

Tegler snorted. "I got a real good look at her, if you remember."

"That ain't what I'm talkin' about," Tegler's man said.

"Then what the hell are you talkin' about?"

"You know when she struck her head against the edge of the buildin'?"

"Yeah."

"Well, I think it killed her."

"What?"

Tegler and Belle had struggled, Tegler losing his patience and throwing her against the building.

"That's what I'm talkin' about. Go look at her. Randy tried to get a pulse but he couldn't. I think she's dead, Tegler. I think you killed her."

A panic overtook Tegler just then. He had made a career of killing men. But women were a different matter. Sometimes the law let you slide when you just killed other men. But killing women . . . that was a sure way to get yourself hanged.

Tegler went to look at Belle's seminude body sprawled in the shadows of the alley where he'd left after raping her.

He did not like what he saw.

Chapter Twenty-four

Arthur Hunt knew something was wrong. It was on the beard-stubbled face of Lymon Tegler. It was in the anxious way his men kept glancing back at the alley behind them.

"How'd it go with your friend the sheriff?" Tegler asked.

Hunt avoided his sarcasm, instead looking at the deep shadows of the alley.

"What happened?" he asked.

"What?"

"You heard me, Tegler. Something happened."

"What're you, a mind reader?"

Hunt moved two threatening steps closer to Tegler. Many times during their long relationship, Hunt had been tempted to slap the smirk off Tegler's face. Tonight he decided he just might do it.

To one of Tegler's men, he said, "What happened, Shorty?"

Shorty's features were lost in the moonlit shadows. All Hunt could see was how Shorty's eyes flicked nervously to his boss.

"I better tell him, boss," Shorty said.

"You shut up," Tegler said. Then he grinned at Hunt. "I'll tell him." He paused, wiping a hand across his mouth. "You know how Belle was givin' you trouble there at the end?"

Hunt nodded, baffled by where this conversation might be going. What the hell did Belle have to do with anything?

"Well she ain't gonna be botherin' you no more," Tegler said.

Hunt followed Tegler's gaze into the alley. In the moonlight, the dusty floor of the narrow passageway was silver. Hunt stepped around Tegler and looked down the alley. A crumpled form could be seen propped up against a wall.

"Is that Belle?" Hunt said, mind and heart racing. What the hell was going on here?

"Sure is," Tegler said, and grinned. "And she was just about as good as I expected her to be."

Long years of rage went into Hunt's punch. It met solidly with Tegler's chin, smashing bone so hard that it knocked Tegler several feet backward, into the edge of the building behind him.

Hunt then stepped over and kicked the fallen man hard in the ribs.

As Hunt moved for the alleyway, Tegler's

men fanned out, giving him a clear passage. The closer he drew to Belle, the worse he felt.

In the past few weeks, Hunt had come to see that the young woman he'd seemed to fall in love with could not hold his attention for long. He loved her, he supposed, in some frenzied way that mixed passion and vanity but he did not find her interesting.

More and more Hunt had begun fondly recalling his days with Belle. While she was no longer the beauty she'd been, she was the only person with whom Hunt had felt comfortable and willing to confide his secrets.

And now Tegler had —

Rushing to Belle, Hunt dropped to one knee, picked up her arm, and began feeling for a pulse.

The feel of her skin was curious — cold yet sweaty.

There was no pulse.

Desperately, he put his thumb to her neck and felt for a pulse there.

Faintly, he felt one.

He moved closer, putting his head to her bosom. Tegler had ripped away her dress. He wanted to go back and work on Tegler some more.

He raised her head and shouted to the

men at the head of the alley. "Go get the doc and hurry."

Two of the men departed immediately.

Hunt looked back down at Belle. He did not know who to feel sorrier for, her or himself.

He needed to concentrate on breaking Jeremy out of jail. Only by killing Jeremy would the ranch be all his own.

But now things were confused with Belle being —

For a terrible second, he had the sense that the woman he held in his arms was dead.

To reassure himself, he touched her neck once again.

If anything, the pulse was even fainter than before.

Where the hell was that doc?

What could be keeping him?

He lay her back against the ground, taking off his vest and placing it beneath her head as a pillow.

Where the hell was that doc?

Chapter Twenty-five

When she got back to his cell, he was asleep. In the light through the barred window she could see where he'd been wounded. His hair tousled, his hands steepled beneath his head, he looked like a young boy.

Lisa stood there long moments, watching him fondly. She had waited so many long and hopeless hours to tell him this. But now, curiously, instead of excitement, she felt a kind of dread.

How would he take her words?

Oh, certainly he would be happy that he was no longer a suspect in the Dane girl's murder.

But how about the news of his father?

How would anybody react when he learned that his father had killed his mother and then tried to frame him for murder?

Taking the key that Cage had given her, she quietly opened the cell, easing back that door that needed oiling, went in and sat down gently on the bed next to him.

At first, she did not speak, only stroked

his head. Jeremy had always needed protection, which was one of the traits she liked about him. Unlike other men, Jeremy evoked a vast tenderness in her. She supposed this wasn't what most women felt when they spoke of romantic love but it was the kind of love she wanted to feel for a man.

"Jeremy."

Her voice was soft as the shadows here in the chill damp gloom of the cell.

"Jeremy."

Her breath touched his cheeks as softly as her hand touched his hair.

"Jeremy."

He stirred, mumbling something lost to her.

She leaned down and kissed him on the forehead.

One eye opened and looked at her. At first, he did not seem to know who she was.

She smiled.

"Sleepy boy," she said.

"How did you get in here?"

She held up the key.

"Cage gave it to me."

"Why would he do something like that?"

"Because you're free."

"I am?"

She nodded. "Sam told Cage who really killed Sally Dane."

"He did?"

"Yes."

"Who was it?"

She averted her eyes.

He sat up, the stiff woolen jail blanket rustling beneath him. He took her arms gently. "Who killed her, Lisa?"

"Your father."

"I don't believe that."

Might as well say it, she thought. Might as well get it over with. "And he also killed —"

But somehow the words caught in her throat.

How could she tell him?

It would destroy him.

"He also killed who?"

"Oh, Jeremy," she said, and fell into his arms, wanting at the same time to hold him and be held.

But Jeremy wanted to know. He held her away from him, looking straight into her eyes. "He also killed who?"

"I don't want to say it, Jeremy. You may never forgive me for saying it."

"Tell me."

"Your mother."

"What?"

"Sam says that your father killed your mother."

"That's a lie."

"That's what Sam says."

"She died in a fire."

"Sam says that your father knocked her out first and then set the fire."

"Sam's always been jealous of my father."

"Think, Jeremy."

"About what?"

"About how she died."

"What about it?"

"Haven't you ever wondered? Haven't you ever had doubts?"

"No." He shook his head. "And why would my father kill Sally Dane and then try to blame me."

"If you're dead, he gets the ranch."

"He's my father. We haven't always gotten along but he loves me."

"Does he?"

"You don't have any right to talk this way. Not about my own father."

She pulled him to her then and put her face deep into his shoulder. She knew they were beyond words now. She also knew that she had perhaps destroyed their relationship forever.

She should not have told him. . . .

And then he startled her.

There in the darkness, pressed so close to her she could smell the sleep on him, he began crying.

Not sobbing the way a woman does.

But in the halting, hesitant, uncertain way a man cries.

And she knew then that he did, in fact, believe her.

"I'm sorry, Jeremy," she said.

He put his face into her shoulder now.

She let him cry. She stroked the back of his head.

"I'm sorry," she said again.

"I guess I always suspected it," he said. "But killing my mother — my God."

"Cage is going to arrest him."

"My father won't give up."

"Cage will kill him then."

He said nothing. Let her words lay on the air. Then, "I want to kill him."

"No. Leave things to Cage."

"I owe my mother that."

"Please, Jeremy. Think of us. Our future."

"But my mother —"

She held him tighter, stroked his head again, tried to gentle him the way she would gentle an animal. "Please, Jeremy," she said there in the darkness. "Please."

"She's dead, Art."

"The hell."

"I'm afraid it's the truth."

Arthur Hunt was wild within himself. "I got a pulse just a few minutes ago."

"Maybe you did a few minutes ago but not now."

The doc stood to the right of Belle. Hunt stood to the left.

"What the hell happened here, anyway?" the doc asked, indicating how her clothes had been torn.

"Something I'm going to take care of." Hunt's gaze went up to the head of the alley.

Tegler was on his feet, walking around, glowering down at Art.

That was the way Art wanted it.

"Cover her up, doc," Hunt said, not taking his eyes from Tegler.

"Take her over to the funeral home?"

"Fine."

"You better calm down, Art. Lot of things you should be thinking over."

"You just get her over to the funeral parlor. Let me worry about the rest."

The doc nodded. He took off his black suitcoat and bent over to place it across Belle's dead body.

Arthur Hunt went up to the head of the alley where Tegler stood, flanked by his men.

"You boys stand back," Hunt said.

"Don't try anything crazy, Art," Tegler said. "You got me good enough already. Slammin' my head like that."

"She's dead."

"I didn't kill her on purpose."

"Maybe not on purpose but the result was the same."

"You was done with her anyway."

Hunt got Tegler a clean fast slap across the mouth.

"Now you get ready," Hunt said.

Tegler's hands dropped to the guns on his shell belt. "Don't have to be this way, Art."

"Yeah it does."

"She was a whore."

"She was what she was."

"I didn't mean to kill her, Art. You ain't takin' that into account. And beside —" Tegler was now ready to tell Hunt about the letter he'd found on Belle.

"Shut up!" Hunt said. "I'm sick of your mouth!"

The men around Tegler eased away from their boss. The gunfight was now inevitable. Standing too close was an easy way to die.

Hunt's hand dropped to his holster. "Any time, Tegler."

"You know what I heard, Art?"

"I don't care what you heard."

"One of the boys said your cousin Sam was over to the jail and told that Cage everything." He grinned. "They caught you, Art. They know about that whore you killed and they know you killed your wife, too."

"Any time, Tegler."

"You won't even get out of this town, Art. You won't even —"

In the moonlight shadows, at the head of the dusty alley, a black cat crossing just back of Tegler, Hunt went for his .44.

The shot blasted through the darkness, a ragged flame of fire exploding from the gun's bore, and moments later there was a small scream as Tegler twisted slowly to the ground, his Colt falling in a flurry of silver to the dust below.

"You killed him, Mr. Hunt," said one of the men. "You killed him for sure."

Hunt shoved his gun back in his holster and walked back down the alley, where the doc was just finishing with Belle. Now that she was covered up, the doc was going to get the mortician and his wagon.

"You ain't got enough trouble without

killin' somebody else?" the doc said, looking up from Belle's corpse.

"You don't think he needed killing?"

"Not right now. And not by you. You ever heard of law and order, Hunt? That's what we got lawmen for."

"Just go get the mortician."

"You ain't my boss, Hunt, and don't start makin' like you are, you understand?"

The doc was known for his pride. Hunt had offended him.

"I don't want her to lay out here and let the animals get at her," Hunt said, his voice gentle now.

The doc nodded and went off and got the mortician.

Hunt had somewhere to go, too.

Now that it was all coming down around him — he had no doubt that Tegler had told the truth, that cousin Sam had told everything to Cage — he did not plan to leave town empty-handed.

Even though it was just a little after 2 a.m., Hunt was going to withdraw some money from the bank.

Chapter Twenty-six

Cage had stepped out on the boardwalk to roll himself a cigarette and inhale some of the chill night air. As the night turned now toward dawn, the sky was streaked with lighter patches of blue. Despite his edge of anxiety, Cage yawned.

Then he heard the gunshots. They came from the east end of town.

Within moments, Sorenson rushed outside, clutching a carbine. "Wonder what's goin' on."

"Only one way we're going to find out," Cage said, hurrying back inside to get his own carbine.

Jeremy sat in the front office. In the chair next to him was Lisa. She held his hand.

"What happened?" Jeremy said.

"Don't know yet."

"I'd like to go with you."

"Me, too," John T. Larson said. He started to get up from his own chair but his weakness put him right back down.

"Why don't you both wait here?" Cage said. He smiled and nodded to the cell block. "We can't leave a dangerous criminal like Sam Jenkins locked up in the back without a guard."

Larson grinned. "I see what you mean." He looked grateful to be sitting down again.

Cage grabbed his carbine and said, "I can't stop you and Jeremy from going where you want, Miss Tate. But if you want my advice, I'd stay right here till we get all this resolved. We don't have any idea where Hunt is — or his men."

"I'd still like to go with you," Jeremy said.

"Maybe later," Cage said. "Now I've got to get going."

As they made their way down the empty street, Cage kept scanning the darkened buildings for any sign of a gun barrel glinting off the murky streetlight.

Cage listened closely for any untoward sound. Hunt's men could easily be hiding out on rooftops, waiting to fire. The gunshots might have been a ploy to get Cage and Sorenson to move away from the office.

As soon as they saw the doc hurrying down the middle of the street, they knew better.

"Where you headed, Doc?" Sorenson called.

"Undertakers."

"Who's dead?"

"Belle."

"Belle?" Cage said. "Who killed her?"

The doc shook his head. "Tegler." He grimaced. "After he got done raping her, that is."

"What was the gunfire all about?"

"Hunt drew down on Tegler. Killed him."

"Where's Hunt now?"

The doc shrugged. "That's a good question. He just took off. Didn't say anything."

"Where are Tegler's men?"

"Up by the body." He pointed to the intersection. "Right around the corner."

"Let's go," Cage said to Sorenson.

He caught a glimpse of Sorenson's eyes. The deputy was rightly concerned about what they were walking into.

Sorenson hefted his carbine and started walking alongside Cage. "Tegler's got some pretty mean men."

He had scarcely finished saying this when a group of men working their horses hard came around the corner. In the lamplight they looked like shadowy ghosts.

But there was nothing ghostly about their gunfire.

As soon as they saw Cage and Sorenson, one of them cried "Lawmen!" and they opened fire.

Cage and Sorenson scarcely had time to duck behind a watering trough before bullets started sending yellow-red flares into the gloom.

Cage got one clean shot off after staying down for half a minute. He got one of the riders right in the face. The man screamed as his horse gave out beneath him.

Sorenson had similar luck.

A rider was fanning out wide to come around left where he could get a good shot at both the men.

Sorenson got him in his sights and dispatched a bullet that exploded the man's chest. He was lifted, as if by a giant hand, right off the back of his horse and hurled to the ground.

Cage took time to smile at his deputy then went back to his shooting.

Gunfire was exchanged for three minutes before anybody else was hit. This time, Sorenson was wounded in the arm. He went over on his back, writhing with the pain but otherwise making no noise.

Cage crawled over to him, bullets flying no more than an inch above his back.

"You all right?"

"Be fine."

"Sure?"

Sorenson nodded. "Kill one of those sonofabitches for me."

Cage grinned. "My pleasure."

By the time another full minute had passed, Cage had managed to kill two of those sonofabitches for Sorenson. One he caught flanking to the right on horseback, the other he caught up on a rooftop across the street.

There were now two left.

The street reeked of gunfire and blood.

Somewhere in the shadows across the street the other two lurked.

One of them made it easy for Cage by firing. The yellow-red flare gave him away.

Cage took a good shot and moments later a man could be heard strangling on his own blood. Cage had apparently shot him in the throat.

Cage was just starting to reload when he heard Sorenson cry out.

Whirling, Cage tried to get his Colts from his holsters but it was too late.

A big, bearded man had stepped from the gloom and was about to shoot Cage.

"I always wanted to kill a sheriff," the man said. He sounded drunk and not quite right in the head. "An' I guess now's my chance."

He stepped closer, over the prone body

of Sorenson, to reach Cage and make sure his shot didn't go awry.

He should have paid closer attention to Sorenson.

The wounded deputy brought his leg straight up, catching the man in the groin.

A howl of pain ricocheted off the dawning sky.

The man fired but it went over Cage's head.

Cage lunged for him, grabbing the man by the beard and slamming his head down against the edge of a trough.

You could feel the life drain from the man.

There under the ripping force of Cage's hand in his beard, the man died from a concussion.

Cage threw him away from the trough into the gloom.

"You better go get the doc," Cage said, helping the deputy to his feet.

Sorenson winced then looked at the bodies strewn all over the street. "Sure didn't know you had that kind of violence in you."

Cage smiled. "I guess I didn't know either."

Chapter Twenty-seven

Tisdale was the banker's name. Arthur Hunt had always hated him. Early on, before Hunt had been able to exert his own influence on managing the ranch, Tisdale had continually reminded Hunt that the ranch was his wife's property.

Now, Tisdale's house was dark. Apparently the man hadn't been awakened by the gunfire at the other end of town.

Hunt used the lattice work to climb up to the second floor, where the bedrooms lay. Hunt had been there at several parties and still remembered the layout of the house.

When he reached the second story, he smashed in a window with his fist, felt around inside for the window latch, and then opened the window wide enough to wiggle inside.

He was in the den. Moonlight fell in broken patterns through the eastern window. The aroma of pipe smoke lay sweetly on the air.

Hearing somebody stir down the hall, he

scrambled to his feet, pulled his Colt, and left the room.

In a comic nightgown, Johnathan Tisdale came down the hallway, holding a kerosene lamp in front of him. In the lamplight you could see his jowly face and bourbon-red nose and eyes, which were little more than sleepy slits.

"Evening, Johnathan."

Tisdale started. "Wh— what are you doing in my house, Art?"

"Need to make a little withdrawal. Go put your clothes on."

"My clothes? What for?"

"Because we're going to the bank."

"At this hour?"

He smirked. "Yes, Johnathan, at this hour."

Just then a stout woman in a full-length nightgown that matched Tisdale's appeared in the doorway behind her husband. "What's the trouble here, Johnathan?" Then she saw Hunt. "Why, Arthur, what are you doing here?"

"I'm going to kidnap your husband."

"Kidnap him? Are you joshing me, Art?"

"It's nigh on to four-thirty a.m. It's way too late to 'josh' anybody." He waved his gun at her. "Now you get back in there and you won't get hurt."

"Hurt? But Art, we're your friends."

He spat on the floor. "Not anymore, you're not." He pointed the gun dead on at her heart. "You tell her to get back in there, Johnathan, or I'll kill her right here and right now."

"He isn't joshing, honey."

"Of all the things —" she started to say but her husband gave her another warning glance.

She disappeared into the shadows of the bedroom. "You go in after her. I'll wait right outside the door. You've got two minutes to get dressed. Otherwise I empty this gun into the room."

"I can't believe this of you, Art. You were always such a gentleman."

"Oh, yes." Hunt laughed. "That's me all right. Such a gentleman."

He waved the gun again.

"In there."

Tisdale went into his bedroom and began to dress. He wife kept muttering things about what a bad man Arthur Hunt had turned out to be. Tisdale was smart enough to shush her.

Cage said, "I'm looking for Arthur Hunt. You seen him tonight?"

"Earlier," the barkeep said. "But that

was a couple hours ago."

Cage glanced around the saloon. With its sawdust floor and pine-slab bar, the place was obviously intended to withstand the rigors of drunken men who liked to engage in fistfights. At this time of night, the place smelled not only of warm beer and cheap liquor but of vomit and smoke and urine from the nearby outhouse as well.

Cage needed fresh air.

He nodded to the barkeep and went back outside.

Standing under the overhang of the saloon, he rolled his eyes toward the sky. Dawn was now streaking the firmament. Distantly, he could hear cocks crowing.

He had spent the last hour and a half searching the town for Arthur Hunt. He'd had no luck.

Tired, he reached up and touched the badge that rode on his suitcoat. It still felt funny. He had sworn, after leaving his last post, that he would never again wear a badge such as this. Ever.

Now, so early in the morning, the events of this night a jumble, he tried to think back through exactly how he had become involved in this.

He still wondered what kind of man could cold-bloodedly kill his wife and then go on to try and frame his own son for murder.

He tried to attach these thoughts to the man he'd seen earlier. But Arthur Hunt had given no outward signs of being a madman. If anything, he'd looked like nothing more than a middle-aged man who would eventually take on a grand-fatherly look.

He was lost in his thoughts when he heard his name spoken.

"Mr. Cage."

Standing in front of him in the street were Jeremy Hunt and Lisa Tate. Jeremy was still limping from where he'd been wounded in the leg. He appeared remark-ably fit otherwise. Given his age and his health, he'd probably recover much faster than John T. Larson.

Cage nodded.

"Did you find him?" Jeremy said.

"Not so far."

"Oh." Jeremy sounded both disappointed and relieved.

Lisa frowned. "You know what he's afraid of, Mr. Cage?"

"What?"

"That you'll kill him. Even after he killed his own wife and tried to arrange things so Jeremy would hang — Jeremy still doesn't want anything bad to happen to him."

"I just want to talk to him before —"
Jeremy shook his head, as if ridding his
mind of a terrible thought. He looked at
Lisa. "He's still my father, Lisa, whether
we like it or not."

"You don't owe him anything."

"No," Jeremy said. "No, I don't but —"

Cage could hear that this was an argu-
ment of long standing. He could also hear
that it would likely never be resolved. At
least not by Jeremy.

Despite all the things he'd done to
Jeremy, Arthur Hunt remained the young
man's blood parent. That was a bond that
virtually nothing could break. Nothing.

"You'll give him a chance? I mean you
won't just start shooting?" Jeremy said.

"Not unless he forces me to."

"I'd like to go with you."

"Oh Jeremy, let Mr. Cage handle
things," Lisa said. "We can wait over at the
restaurant."

"You don't have any idea where he'd
hide out in town here?" Cage asked.

Jeremy shook his head. "No."

"No close friends you can think of?"

Jeremy smiled bitterly. "My father isn't a
man who appreciates having good friends."

Cage nodded and stepped down off the

walk in front of the saloon.

He raised the carbine then tucked it between his arm and torso. "Lisa's right. Why don't you wait at the restaurant. We'll find him soon enough."

"Maybe he left town."

"His horse was still by the livery. If he left, it would have been on foot, and that's pretty unlikely."

Jeremy stared at the carbine. "Remember what I asked, Mr. Cage, all right? About not shooting first?" He sounded plaintive, like a young child begging.

Blood was stronger than just about anything Cage could think of.

"I'll remember, Jeremy," Cage said softly. He looked at Lisa. "Now why don't you take Jeremy over and buy him some breakfast?"

Lisa clutched Jeremy's arm. "That sounds like a wonderful idea."

Cage watched her help Jeremy down the street. The limp made him look almost pathetic.

"You're not going to shoot me, are you, Art?"

"Depends."

"On what?"

"On whether you cooperate."

"Oh, I'll cooperate, Art. You can bank on it."

" 'Bank' on it. That's pretty funny."

"Yes, I see what you mean." Tisdale tried to laugh. The sound came out short and ugly.

They stood in the alley behind the bank. Hunt had his Colt pressed tightly against Tisdale's head. "Open the door."

"You promise not to shoot me, Art? My wife — she'd never forgive me if you shot me."

"I'll keep that in mind, Johnathan. Now open the door."

"All right, Art." Tisdale was starting to tremble again. The sight disgusted Hunt. He looked away.

Tisdale was trembling so hard now that the key clanked to the concrete step.

"Sorry," Tisdale said.

When he bent over to take the key, he had an accident in his pants. "Oh, my God," he said.

The odor was fetid.

"You're some piece of work," Hunt said. "Some piece of work all right."

Tisdale tried the key again.

It took her twenty-eight minutes to work her way out of the rope with which Hunt had lashed her to the kitchen chair.

She was so mad at Arthur she could spit.

Even though she'd never considered Hunt — or his wife for that matter — social equals, she'd been forced by business necessity to invite him to her home. To eat her canapés. To gaze on her watercolors imported from France. To listen to viola concerts.

But did Arthur Hunt appreciate any of it?

Hardly.

He'd kidnapped her husband. Tied her to a chair. And in the course of these things, had taken every opportunity to insult her.

Even if Arthur Hunt somehow managed to escape the gallows and become once again the richest rancher in the county, it would be a cold day in Hades before he'd ever again dine on her canapés or bend an ear to her viola concerts.

She ran from the house shrieking, running down the center of the street toward town.

Windows were tugged up and heads gaped out.

But she was too hysterical to stop and ask for help.

The only time she managed to shriek out

something intelligible was when she said to Adams, owner of the local lumberyard and an important figure in country club politics, "See if he ever gets my canapés again."

Adams had no idea what the hell she was talking about and promptly went back to bed so he could continue fondling his wife's backside in hopes that she would, for once, give in and honor him with a "morning gift."

Meanwhile, Mrs. Johnathan Tisdale continued running down the center of the street.

"I want half a million dollars."

"But that's not fair."

"What the hell are you talking about?"

"You've only got slightly less than a quarter of a million on deposit here."

"So?"

"So that's all you're entitled to."

Hunt sighed deeply. "You don't seem to understand, Johnathan."

"Understand what?"

"I'm robbing this place."

"What?"

"I'm taking all the money I want and loading it on the buckboard I brought around back."

"But you're only entitled to what you have on deposit."

"You want to get shot, Johnathan?"

Tisdale gulped. "All I'm asking is that you be fair."

"Would the Dalton boys be fair?"

"Pardon me?"

"If the Daltons came in here and stuck up your bank, would they be fair? Take only what they were 'entitled' to?"

"I guess not."

"Then pretend I'm the Dalton boys."

They stood in the center of the bank lobby. The plush, heavy curtains muffled their voices. The place smelled sweetly of furniture polish from its cleaning last night.

"Go on."

"But Art, do you have any idea what the depositors will say?"

"I know what they'll say if you get killed. They'll say, 'Poor Johnathan. Too god damn dumb to open the vault the way Hunt wanted him to.'"

"But bank money isn't *my* money."

"You're right, Johnathan. Now it's my money. Now get moving."

Hunt jabbed him with the Colt.

Johnathan staggered forward, toward the vault.

He tripped and fell face first against the vault.

"You know the combination," Hunt said. "Now go ahead."

"Are you sure you won't reconsider, Art? You've got your reputation to think of, you know."

Hunt smiled. "That's what I'm worried about all right, Johnathan. My reputation."

He cocked the Colt.

"Now open that door or I'll kill you."

Chapter Twenty-eight

Cage was walking through an alley, searching the buildings, when he heard the screaming.

He started running immediately, down to the head of the alley and then to the right. The town was just now coming awake, a milk wagon clattering down the street, dogs barking, and the first sign of little kids coming out to play long before the dew had dried on the grass.

Cage found the woman running straight down the middle of the street.

He had no idea who she was, only that something terrible had befallen her. She wore a long nightie, her hair was rolled up into curlers, and she kept waving her arms and staring at her hands.

Cage got along beside her and reined her in the way he would have a horse.

"He took my husband," she said. He could see that she was hysterical.

As she shook her hands — almost as if she were trying to get rid of them — Cage looked at her wrists.

Rope burns had left deep raw indentations in the flesh.

"What happened to your wrists?"

"He tied me up."

"Who tied you up?"

"Arthur Hunt."

The name had the effect of a shot on Cage. "Where is he?"

"The bank."

"What's he doing there?"

She shook her head and gulped. She was trying to calm herself, gather herself enough so that she could talk coherently.

"He wants my husband to open the vault."

"You go over to the office. John T. is there and he'll give you some coffee."

"I'm afraid for Mr. Tisdale."

"Who's Mr. Tisdale?"

"Why my husband, of course."

Pretty odd that she would refer to her own husband as "Mr.," Cage thought.

"What about him?"

"When he gets frightened, he gets asthma attacks."

"Oh."

"And he was petrified. The way Arthur Hunt kept poking him with that gun. Petrified."

"I need to be going now, ma'am."

"If you see Mr. Tisdale, tell him I love him and that I'm praying for him."

"Yes, ma'am."

"And tell him I'll make rhubarb pie for dinner tonight."

"Yes, ma'am."

"If he's alive, that is."

And then she started noisy bawling.

Cage ran over to the bank, carbine ready.

In less than ten minutes, Arthur Hunt loaded sixteen bags of currency on to the buckboard he'd taken from the livery.

Not that he'd done any of the actual work himself.

He'd made Johnathan Tisdale do it and that was quite a sight.

Tisdale, sweat streaming down his face, brought the last bag out and said, "I need a rest, Art. I can't help it." His chest was heaving and an asthmatic rattle was starting in his throat. "Please."

"Hop up here with me and sit down."

Tisdale looked as if he was being tricked.

"Really?" he asked.

"Really. Get up here."

Tisdale put out a hand. Hunt helped him up.

"I really appreciate this," Tisdale said,

his lungs sounding like rusty accordions. "All the excitement's really getting to my asthma."

In a single, swift motion Hunt brought the shiny Colt to Tisdale's head and eased back the hammer.

"Wh— what're you doing?" Tisdale said, sweat coming in fat silver globules now.

"Look up there."

Tisdale raised his head and saw Cage at the head of the alley.

Cage had been running. Now he stopped.

Hunt called out, "Unless you drop that carbine, Mr. Cage, I'm going to put a bullet in Tisdale's head right now."

"You don't have a chance of getting out of town," Cage called.

"Of course I do," Hunt said, sounding almost merry. "That's because I've got Tisdale here sitting next to me."

Cage shook his head in both disgust and anger and eased his carbine flat to the ground.

"Now you back out of the alley out on the street," Hunt said.

Cage said, "Mr. Tisdale, don't you try anything brave."

Hunt laughed. "I don't think you have to worry about that, Mr. Cage."

Hunt tightened the reins in his hand and started the wagon out of the alley. The traces and the heavy wheels and the axles made a formidable noise in the dawn stillness.

Just before he reached the head of the alley, Hunt got the horses going fast so that when the wagon rounded the corner Cage wouldn't have time to gather himself.

Cage knelt in the middle of the street, a Colt stuck in his hand.

Hunt got the horses running even faster — directly for Cage.

Hunt knew that Cage wouldn't dare fire, not with Tisdale aboard.

But just before he reached Cage, he shoved Tisdale out of the wagon and on to the ground.

Then he opened fire on Cage, forcing the lawman to pitch himself to the ground.

Hunt kept the buckboard running right for the lawman.

Cage barely rolled out of the way before the heavy wheels rumbled over the ground where he had just been.

Cage saw a horse hitched to the post outside one of the saloons. Dust flying from his clothes, he ran over and mounted it. He certainly would have wished for a better horse than this one but right now he didn't have much choice but to take it.

Far ahead, the wagon lost in its own road dust, Hunt was flying back to his ranch.

Once there, he would have no trouble escaping. His men could hold off the law until Hunt was long gone.

Behind him now, Cage heard shod hooves. As he turned around, he saw Jeremy Hunt come riding toward him on a bay.

"I'm going with you," Jeremy called.

"You sure you want to?"

"Absolutely. He's my father."

Cage shook his head and together they rode on.

Chapter Twenty-nine

In five minutes, Cage and Jeremy had pulled within firing distance of the wagon.

Hard as Arthur Hunt pressed the horses, the buckboard was too much to pull while maintaining anywhere near top speed.

The buckboard lumbered along toward a rocky incline that slowed it even more.

Cage pulled his carbine and prepared to fire.

He was about to get a shot off, when Jeremy reached across his mount and pushed the gun away.

"Let me talk to him," Jeremy shouted over the dust and the hoofbeats. "I don't want to kill him unless we have to."

"Kid, he was willing to see you hang for a murder you didn't commit. You can't talk any sense to that man."

Jeremy said, "I'm going to try."

Jeremy pulled away from Cage, pressing his mount even harder.

In moments, he was alongside the wagon, the blind side where his father's gunshots could not reach.

Now that the buckboard was on the hill, the pace had slowed considerably.

Over the clatter and clamor of the wagon, Jeremy shouted, "I want to talk to you."

His father gawked around the edge of the wagon. "Get out of here, Jeremy."

Jeremy shook his head and pulled even closer to the wagon. He had to shout to be heard. "I know you were going to watch me hang. I've accepted that. But I don't believe what they tell me about my mother. You really didn't kill her, did you?"

But Jeremy saw instantly that it was true.

His father could not meet his gaze. "Go on," Arthur Hunt said. "Get out of here."

"How could you?" Jeremy said. "She was your wife."

His father stared at him a long moment then frowned. "Things happen to people, Jeremy. I don't expect you to understand."

Almost without realizing it, Jeremy raised his .44 and aimed it at his father's head.

"I owe you this, father."

Hunt shrugged. "I can't disagree with you there, son."

But before Jeremy fully understood what was happening, Hunt produced a Colt from his lap and fired at Jeremy.

The bouncing mount made Jeremy a moving target so all the bullets did was knock him from his horse. None of the shots landed.

Hunt had come to the top of the grade now and, on the downside, was picking up speed.

Seeing what had happened, Cage spurred his horse and went after Hunt.

Looking over the fallen Jeremy to see if he was all right, Cage said, "I'm probably going to have to kill him, kid."

Jeremy looked as if he didn't know what to think. He seemed angry and sad both. But mostly he just seemed confused.

Hunt's first shot nearly knocked Cage to the ground.

Cage had to duck down along the side of the bay in order to get close enough to shoot.

His first two shots went wild, came no-where near to catching Hunt.

Soon enough, Hunt returned fire.

On the third shot, Cage's bay buckled, dumping him in the dust.

Fortunate that neither he nor the bay had broken any bones, Cage scrambled to his feet and began running down the in-cline until he saw that he would never catch up with the buckboard.

Eyes scanning the valley below, Cage saw that the buckboard would soon have to negotiate a tight left turn, putting the wagon straight in front of him though at some distance.

He would have one or at most two clear shots at the wagon as it was turning.

Dropping to one knee, Cage prepared himself. The dust generated by the rumbling wagon made Cage's shot even more difficult.

Ten-nine-eight . . .

He waited, watching.

He was trembling.

Five-four-three . . .

The wagon was turning, turning . . .

His finger tightened on the trigger.

He squinted.

Ready.

Set.

He pulled back the trigger.

Once.

Twice.

At first, he thought he'd missed.

The wagon rumbled on through the dust at considerable speed.

But then he saw, where the curve broke to the right again, that the horses had no guidance.

They ran right off the road and over the edge of a steep gulley.

You could hear the horses crying even from here.

The force of the buckboard smashing into the ravine below shook the ground beneath Cage.

There could be little doubt about what had happened to Arthur Hunt.

Cage went back to see how Jeremy Hunt was doing.

Chapter Thirty

Next morning, at the train station, three of the people who saw Cage off bore the signs of the past twenty-four hours. John T. Larson, Ron Sorenson, and Jeremy Hunt were all bandaged up in some way.

Only Lisa Tate looked fresh and whole.

"You sure did a good job," John T. Larson said. He smiled. "Probably not as good a job as I could've done but —"

Sorenson laughed. "You did a fine job, Cage. I enjoyed working with you."

Jeremy put out his hand. Cage shook it. "I appreciate everything, Mr. Cage. That is —" He looked at Lisa. "We appreciate everything."

"We certainly do," Lisa said.

"You won't reconsider?" Larson said.

Cage shook his head. "My law enforcement days are behind me. I wired my brother. He's expecting me." He nodded and touched the empty space where ordinarily his badge would have gone. He would never forget the fact that his deputy had been killed. Nor would he ever know if his own shortcomings had been responsible for the deputy's death.

But that was the past.

Ahead lay the future, Yuma and ranching. He would keep packing his two guns — but in the hope he'd never have to use them for anything more uncivilized than target shooting.

He boarded the train, turning back only once to look at them. "You've got a nice town here. You're lucky people."

Then Cage disappeared inside the Pullman and was gone forever.